What would you do if your best friend told the entire sixth grade that the vice-principal called you down to his office because you'd left a mash note on his Datsun? And it wasn't true. You'd moan, "Rachel Vellars, how could you?" the same way Cory Matthewson did.

As Cory embarks on some new friendships, things begin to change—but not always for the better. After a few roller-coaster weeks, Cory learns some important lessons about friends.

Rachel Vellars, How Could You?

Lois I. Fisher

DODD, MEAD & COMPANY
New York

3   4   5   6   7   8   9   10

Library of Congress Cataloging in Publication Data

Fisher, Lois I.
Rachel Vellars, how could you?

Summary: Eleven-year-old Cory changes schools when
she goes to live with her father after her parents'
divorce, and has some adjustments to make in choosing and
holding friendships.
[1. Friendship—Fiction.   2. Single-parent family—
Fiction.   3. Divorce—Fiction]   I. Title.
PZ7.F5338Rac   1984   [Fic]   83-27481
ISBN 0-396-08327-7
ISBN 0-396-08741-8 (pbk.)

To Mama and Dad,
for their continued support

Chapter 1

For a third time, the phone rang in the vice-principal's inner office. I squirmed on the soft-cushioned chair. The eighth-grade monitor smirked. One could always spot an eighth grader at Markham. They had superior airs and wore their green-and-gold sweaters with a flair, the kind of flair my mom had with clothes.

"You'll have to wait some more," the monitor whined. "Mr. Delancey is on the phone again."

I nodded. My voice was stuck somewhere between my rib cage and throat. Never in my whole life, all eleven-and-a-half years of it, had I been called to the vice-principal's office. I never caused trouble. I wasn't like Rachel Vellars, my best (and only) friend, who slid in and out of trouble the way I slid in and out of second base.

How would Rachel have handled all this? First, I concentrated on the way I'd acted.

The smug monitor had wiggled into Mrs. Albert's first period history class. We were discussing Russian tsars. Markham school has a neat curriculum; I think the teachers make it up as they go along. It's a lot better than P.S. 599 in Manhattan where we never got beyond the capitals of the fifty states. Anyhow, she wiggled in and handed Mrs. Albert a folded note. In a real surprised voice, the teacher said, "Cory Matthewson, Mr. Delancey would like to see you in his office."

Now I get good grades in history, but I don't volunteer answers much or do projects for extra credit. I also don't cause a lick of trouble. So I blushed, slowly got to my feet, and managed to drop my notebook. The kids laughed. I reddened more. Then I followed the monitor out, down here, where she ordered me to "Sit!" in a tone used to command an Irish setter. I sat and listened to the phone ring. That's me. What about Rachel?

When Mrs. Albert announced that Mr. Delancey wanted to see Rachel—in a totally unsurprised voice since Rachel is called out of her class plenty of times—Rachel would have hooted. "Me? He wants me again? Boy, I think that good-looking guy has a huge crush on yours truly." Then she would have stood and knocked everything off her desk, just for dramatic effect. She'd march out with the eighth grader, swiveling her own big hips in a gross imitation of the monitor. When she arrived in the office, she wouldn't have waited. She'd have barged in and said, "What's happening, Mr. D? Why am I here again?" She was not a stranger to this office.

I sighed. The monitor glared. I quickly looked around at my surroundings. Markham sure didn't look anything like old P.S. 599, probably because my former school had been built as a school. Markham started out life in the 1920s as a speakeasy. That's the name for a nightclub that sold illegal liquor during Prohibition (another interesting topic Mrs. Albert had covered). When Prohibition ended, it became a regular nightclub with gambling upstairs, then a boarding-house, followed by an office building, then abandoned until the Markham group bought it for a private school. All the rooms were different sizes. There were archways, a huge marble lobby, and steps and stair-cases where you least expected them. Even the bath-rooms were fancy.

After seven months, I still wasn't used to it. But I loved it. It was the greatest school Daddy could have found. I only wished that everyone in the sixth grade thought of me the way I thought about the school.

I tugged at my short blond hair. Why couldn't it be long and silky like Beth Lowery's? Then when I got nervous (like now), I could twirl my hair and make lovely soft curls instead of forming sweaty cowlicks. My hair is baby fine and needs a pixie cut to make it look more appealing than yellow seaweed. I also have a heart-shaped face and wear silver-rimmed glasses when I read, which is a lot.

"Go in now, Cory Matthewson," the monitor said. Her large green eyes flickered and she reminded me of Amanda Fitzgibbons, one of Beth's best friends. They formed two-thirds of the sixth-grade leader group. Everyone looked up to them.

Mr. Delancey was off the phone. He was rubbing his reddish sideburns. The girls giggle over him constantly. I don't know why; he's older than my father!

"Cory?"

"Yes." I was glad to learn I still had a voice.

He didn't ask me to sit, which I took as a bad sign. He smiled, though, which wasn't bad. He leaned over the side of his modular desk. All faculty members have modular desks and nearly all of them have terminals on them. Mr. Delancey's did. Daddy sold them the computers. That's how he first heard of Markham.

"I have something for you."

The way he reached beneath the computer terminal, I thought he was going to give me a floppy disk. But he came up with something quite different. A brown paper bag.

"My lunch?" I squeaked.

"Yes, your father dropped it off. He couldn't remember the names of any of your teachers, but he remembered me because, in addition to being vice-principal, I buy supplies." He gestured to the machine.

My stomach danced (it usually does *something* when I'm nervous), my knees turned to overcooked spaghetti, and I wondered if I'd faint. I'd been summoned to the vice-principal's office to pick up my lunch! Why hadn't the monitor simply delivered it instead of making me trek all the way down here, wait through three phone calls, and take at least ten years off my young and delicate life?

Mr. Delancey seemed to read my thoughts. "I wanted to meet you, Cory. You've been in Markham since October and this is the first time we've had an opportunity to meet. I was going over your records and was delighted with what I discovered. Wonderful grades. No discipline problems. You like us then?"

"Very much."

"Good." He glanced at his digital watch. "You'd better return to class. What's left of it."

"Yes, and um, thank you for this," I said, grabbing the bag.

"You're quite welcome, Cory. Louisa will escort you back."

Louisa. Amanda Fitzgibbons was always whispering about her sister, Lou, and her boyfriends. I eavesdrop when Rachel's quiet for two seconds.

The bell ending the first period clanged before we reached the stairs. "That's it," Louisa said. "You go the rest of the way alone. I have gymnastics next and I'm not about to miss a turn on the mat." And she wiggled off.

I didn't mind going the rest of the way alone. In fact, I ran. I'm pretty fast, which is why stealing bases is my strong point.

As I'd expected, Rachel was slouched in front of Mrs. Albert's room. Rachel's hunter green blazer (except for eighth graders, everyone has to wear blazers and vests) was open, her gold vest was missing a button, another dangled dangerously, and her skirt was wrinkled. When she left the apartment, she was pretty much together. Somewhere between the elevator and homeroom, she starts coming apart, like a knitting project with dropped stitches. By afternoon, that second button would be lost and her much-sewed hem would sag. The other girls sniffed around her like she smelled bad. But Rachel didn't give off any foul odor like Tommy O'Brien did; he splashed along the banks of the Hudson with his Dalmatian. In fact, Rachel always smelled of bubble bath. We're both bubble bath freaks. We exchange new scents all the time.

She suddenly came to life when she spotted me. "What happened?" She wiped her face and it got smudged with purple ink. "You *finally* got into some real trouble, huh?" Her voice boomed off the high lemon-colored ceiling.

I hesitated. Kids were hanging around. Second period for sixth graders is science, which is just three doors down from history. The kids looked at me funny. That was natural. Cory Matthewson, who barely said boo in class—and whose only claim to fame was her base stealing ability, a little bunting, and a good eye for a base on balls—had been summoned to *the* office. It wasn't weird for them to be curious. But why didn't someone ask me what had happened?

Rachel did. "What happened, kiddo? Is it real low-down bad?"

I whispered, "I forgot my lunch."

"You what?"

"I forgot my lunch," I repeated, knowing full well that beagle-eared Rachel heard me the first time.

"Oh, gross! What a dumb thing to do! Did your old

man bring it here?" I nodded. "He is something else, the way he worries about you. Well, it's a good thing I told the kids what I did then."

"What did you tell them?"

"That you left a mash note on Delancey's Datsun."

I blinked and felt myself redden again. Hoarsely, I demanded, "Rachel Vellers, how could you?"

Chapter 2

Incidents like this make me wonder why I'm friends with Rachel. She has a knack for saying and doing the most outrageous things. A mash note on Delancey's Datsun! If she'd made that up about someone else, I would have laughed. But when she made it up about me, I felt awful. I was her best friend. Her *only* friend. Yet, I couldn't stay angry with her. When it came right down to it, getting called to Delancey's office for putting a lovey-dovey note on his car was more exciting than the real story. In fact, the truth was embarrassing. I'm eleven-and-a-half years old. I wouldn't have gone into a panic for forgetting my lunch. I have money with me for pizza or salad or a hamburger. Daddy didn't have to bring the lunch.

So I didn't tell anyone the boring truth. No one else asked me, anyhow.

I wished they had. Tommy talks to me, but he talks

to everyone. Binky Holifax, who plays a terrible third base for our terrible team, discusses rules with me on the field. Off the diamond, he goes on about tropical fish and boa constrictors, not my favorite topics.

Beth sits next to me in English and is my partner in Domestic Arrangements; she chats once in awhile but always about homework or what we're up to in D.A. D.A. is a super class, even if it does have a clunky name. We cook, sew, work on plumbing, learn about fuel bills, and helpful stuff like that.

After school Rachel sat with me in the minibus that drove us back to the Port Hudson condo park. I love where we live. The two buildings that make up the condo park are only six stories high but each takes up half a block. The lawns are beautifully manicured and there's a circular driveway in front of each building. Rachel and I live in the Claredon; Beth lives in the Kingsley. Across from the buildings is a lovely park that has a couple of tennis courts, a bicycle path, a jogger's lane, and a playground. I rarely go there. Rachel's not much into sports and I hate to go there alone with all the other kids fooling around.

Rachel and I also live on the same floor, the fifth. She has the biggest apartment. It's a duplex that takes up part of the fifth and sixth floors. Her father is an investment broker and has plenty of money. His current wife used to work on Wall Street. Mr. Vellars has been married four times, including to Rachel's mother, who now lives in Kentucky and works with under-privileged kids. Rachel said, "If the old man lost all his dough, maybe my mother would get interested in me." I thought that was sad.

It was also one of the reasons I stayed with Rachel. We both lived with our dads (though mine hasn't re-married), and our mothers aren't that enthused about us. Oh, my mom is a nice lady, a fashion designer in Manhattan, intelligent, a real whirlwind. She just isn't a mom. She doesn't like being one, which is why I live with Dad. He loves me and wants me around.

I sometimes wonder if Rachel's father wants her? He's always off tending to the stock market or playing golf. He rarely pays attention to Rachel. The only person who does, outside of me, is Mrs. Heffernan, our growly building manager. She has an office in the basement and Rachel hangs out there a lot. Less, now that I moved here. Mrs. Heffernan scares most people, my father included, but Rachel thinks she's neat. She overwhelms me a little but I'm getting used to her. The same way I'm used to Rachel.

Rachel wanted me to come over and play video games.

"You know my dad doesn't want me anywhere but home after school."

She stared down at her scuffed loafers. "Cory, don't

be such a baby. He doesn't have to find out."

"Those are the rules."

"What about when you play ball, huh? You don't have to be in the apartment then."

"Because he thinks baseball is a good, healthy activity for me, and besides, Mrs. Winchell drives everyone home."

"Your father is strange, kiddo. Here's a guy who sells computers and yet he doesn't like you playing video games. That doesn't make any sense."

"He's a grown-up, what can I tell you?" I shrugged. We were now on the fifth floor. "Have to go. See you tomorrow."

"Yeah, tomorrow," she sighed and trudged off to her apartment at the opposite end of the long hall. She punched the bell wildly, guaranteed to aggravate her stepmother and terrify the timid housekeeper.

I looked away and quickly let myself into our apartment. How could I tell her the truth? Daddy didn't object to me playing video games. What he doesn't want is me hanging around Rachel too much. That's why he really approves of baseball. I'm with other kids. Daddy would probably let me go other places after school, too, so long as Rachel wasn't around. She attracts trouble the way blinds attract dust.

Our apartment has four rooms. I walked into my

green- and cream-colored bedroom. It's super, twice the size of my sleeping space in Manhattan. My mother had partitioned off an alcove there. It was always dark, since the lone, tiny window faced a brick wall. This room faced east and south and was as bright as could be. I also had a real bed instead of a puny junior love seat. Dad had bought me all antique white furniture, including a desk and a high-backed chair. I even had a big spot saved where I could put a computer. Dad already had a machine in the living room.

I changed from my uniform to a lilac T-shirt and jeans. I flopped on my flowered quilt, took out my glasses, and opened a library book. Every other week, Dad and I make a special trip to the library and stock up. I read so much that I sometimes run out of books. That's okay, though, because Markham has a super library. Right now, I'm reading a mystery set in South America.

I got to the part where the main character learns about a spooky burial ground, when I realized it was time to get dinner ready. Someday, I'd like *real* cooking. We have a microwave and that doesn't seem real to me, not compared to the gas range and oven cooking we do in D.A. Beth is very exact about measurements and oven temperature and little details like that. She always chats about the dishes we prepared. I like Beth. In addition to having great silky hair, she's pleasant and friendly—during class. Oh, she's still polite outside of it, but during D.A., well, it's like we're actually friends. I wish we were. I sighed.

Tonight we were having leftover pot roast, baked potatoes, gravy from a mix, and I chose waxed beans from our huge collection of frozen vegetables. Dad walked in while I was setting the table.

"How's pumpkin?"

I dropped the silverware and gave him a big hug. Although I don't mind being alone, it's terrific when he comes home. Daddy isn't too tall, has the same baby-fine blond hair I do, and a fuzzy beard and moustache. His blue eyes twinkle behind gold-rimmed glasses.

He took two Pepsis from the fridge and in minutes, we sat down to dinner. "Did you get your lunch?" was his first question. He asks lots of questions.

"I wouldn't have starved," I said, mushing butter into my steaming potato. Daddy uses sour cream. Yecch.

"I embarrassed you, eh?"

"At first, you scared me. I mean, getting ordered to Delancey's office. That only happens to kids who get into big trouble, like Rachel or Tommy. Not me."

"I'm sorry I frightened you, Cory. Guess I didn't think it through."

"It turned out okay. Rachel told everyone I left a mash note on Delancey's Datsun and that's why he wanted to see—Daddy, Daddy, are you okay?" He was coughing. He quickly downed some cold soda.

"Rachel told them *that?*" he gasped.

"Yes, I know it's a little far-out, but it's more interesting than the truth."

"I wonder about Rachel Vellars," he muttered.

Here we go again. We have this conversation once a week. Or more.

"I just thought you'd get to know the other kids by now, especially with the Eagles."

I put down my fork. "Daddy, Markham isn't like P.S. 599. It's smaller. The kids have little groups. Even on the baseball team. I don't fit in," I added.

"Hey, pumpkin, I don't want you upset."

"I'm not." Not a whole lot, anyway. "It's just that, you know, I didn't have many friends in Manhattan, either."

"You didn't?" He wasn't around much then since his old job kept him on the road three weeks out of four. Now that he has me full time, he's trying to learn everything at once. It's a hard task for him. And not easy for me, either.

"Just Inez Flores and Ginny McNeil."

"Aha! I do remember Ginny. How could a person forget the kid who brought a Great Dane puppy into our closet-sized apartment? A lamp and an ashtray smashed to the floor." We laughed, then his face grew serious. I stared at my waxed beans. "I still think you could make *other* friends here."

Didn't he realize that I wanted other friends, too? But that I wasn't as outgoing as he or Mom? I was quiet and not the type to join things. The Eagles happened by accident. Mrs. Winchell had us run the bases on a warm February afternoon. I beat all the sixth-grade boys. I wasn't surprised since I played ball in Central Park (with Inez, Ginny, and the Great Dane). Mrs. Winchell insisted I try out for the Eagles. She was desperate for warm bodies. I loved being an Eagle, even if the team was horrible and I hadn't made any new friends. In fact, I nearly lost Rachel, come to think of it.

"If you can't come over to my apartment after school or go anyplace else, I don't see why you can play baseball. It's a dumb game." She sulked for a couple of days. Then she started coming to the practice sessions, then to games. She was my cheering section.

"Cory, don't start crying, please," Daddy's voice brought me back to the present.

"I'm not." But for some silly reason, I was. Tears streamed down my face. Sometimes, I get all confused about what I'm supposed to feel and what I want to feel. Friends would be super, great, wonderful, but if I couldn't have lots of them, why couldn't I at least keep Rachel?

Daddy dabbed my cheeks with a spice-print paper towel. I forced myself to stop; I didn't want to make dinner difficult for him. For ten years, he mostly depended on Mom to look after me. Even if she wasn't that interested in me (I could tell), she was there in body. When he and Mom decided to divorce, she announced that he could have custody of me. I was scared he wouldn't want me either, even though he was always super to me during that one week he was home. But he was *ecstatic!* He had to quit the job as a sales rep for a large computer company. He got a job as a manager of a growing computer store in White Plains. We moved to Port Hudson, which is ten minutes away from the store.

I loved the change and having Daddy as my only parent. Even though Mom had been around all the time, I always got the feeling she was a baby-sitter. Taking care of me was a job, a real chore. She always wanted to be doing something else, sketching, going to fashion shows, or studying fabrics that her friends brought over. I knew she loved me in her own way but never knew exactly what to do with me.

"Of course, you can be friends with Rachel. I'm not

stopping you," Daddy was saying. "And I don't mean to make you unhappy. You'll make friends, pumpkin. You're bright, funny when you allow yourself to be, and you really care about people. Also, I don't think there are many kids who would have adjusted to the divorce as easily as you have."

"It wasn't hard because we're all happier this way."

"That's what I mean, Cory. A lot of kids wouldn't see that. They'd see themselves as uprooted or abandoned by one parent. Frankly, I don't think I would have taken it all so gracefully."

I smiled and scooped piping hot gravy over my three slices of pot roast. Daddy's words made me feel great. He really loved me. And I could keep my best friend, even if he didn't like her and she was my only friend. I needed both.

Chapter 3

"I love lasagna!" Rachel said, rubbing her stomach and wrinkling her vest and skirt at the same time. We were on the elevator. "I love lasagna!" she repeated.

"You sound like Garfield."

"Who? Oh, you mean that comic strip cat. Does he like lasagna?"

"Lives for it," I replied. Rachel doesn't know anything about cats; I do. She also doesn't read the funnies. She swears by the *National Nosybody* and magazines about rock and TV stars. She always asks what I'm reading, though. She's not really interested but she wants me to talk. I don't say much sometimes and silence grates on Rachel's nervous system.

"I know I love the stuff. Mrs. Balducci is supposed to be a super cook. From the size of old fats Frannie, what else do you expect?" Rachel hooted.

Frannie Balducci is the other third of the leader

27

group. Today was our day to prepare her mother's "quick" lasagna recipe in Domestic Arrangements. One week, a student brings in a recipe, then Mrs. Lindsey gathers the ingredients and utensils. The following week, we cook. I liked that part best.

"Will you say something already?" Rachel barked as we walked through the tiled lobby and into the street. "You go off and hide somewhere, like a little mouse. My second stepmother did that. Drove me crazy." Then she twirled around. I stepped aside so a spin wouldn't knock me over. "Feel that breeze, kiddo! It's going to be great kite flying weather."

"Now you sound like Charlie Brown."

"Again with the comics? And you laugh at the *National Nosybody!*"

"Well, the stuff you read to me out of it is funnier than most comics."

She ignored my teasing and asked, "So, do you have a kite, kiddo?"

I have never in my life even flown one. I always envied the kids in Central Park who did. Mom was never interested in kites and Daddy was too busy or not there. Since we moved to Port Hudson, I didn't even think about kites until a couple of weeks ago when Rachel casually mentioned that she couldn't wait to start flying her homemade kites. That floored me.

Rachel isn't athletic or concerned about sports. She's also a disaster area in arts and crafts. She insists she makes her own kites and will show me how. Rachel is never boring.

We boarded the bus along with a few others, including Tommy, Binky, tiny Jenny Chee, and Beth, who ran straight to her seat with Frannie and Amanda. Rachel and I had our own seats, too, in the second row across from the driver.

"I'd be afraid to fly a kite," I said. "It might get devoured by a kite-eating tree, the way Charlie Brown's always does."

Rachel stuck a wad of bubble gum in her mouth. "I dunno about you, kiddo. Comic strips aren't really for kids. They're for adults. I read that in the *National Nosybody*. You're kind of like a premature adult. Ever notice that?"

"All the time." I sighed.

She shrugged and her blazer automatically slipped off one shoulder. "So, wanna help me with my kite today?" she said, chewing the gum real hard. "You promised you'd ask your old man about it. You didn't fink out on me, did you?"

"I can't today. Baseball. Tomorrow." I hadn't asked Daddy. I was afraid of what he'd say and doubly afraid of what Rachel would say when I told her

Daddy said no, which is what I expected him to say.

She didn't seem to notice I hadn't answered her question in full. "Get old Amanda-face. She's wearing perfume."

"Mmmm," I said, sinking into my seat and toying with the spiral of a notebook. Naturally, "old Amanda-face" could hear Rachel. So could the whole bus and probably the man in the Volkswagen Rabbit that pulled alongside the bus.

"She sure is. Take a whiff!" Rachel snorted. I sunk more. "It's the same stuff The Fourth Mrs. Vellars uses. She thinks it's terribly sexy. I wonder who old Amanda-face is trying to seduce? How about Clem?" She pointed to the ancient driver and hooted.

We had reached Markham. Kids started to file out. "Rachel Vellars, how could you?" Amanda said. "I will never speak to you again!"

"You don't usually speak to me now. What's the difference?"

Amanda's huge emerald eyes looked daggers at Rachel, who grinned happily. Clem glared at her when she got off the bus, too. She paused on the curb and called to him, "Look, Amanda-face is the one with the perfume. You're just an innocent bystander, Clem."

"You got to be the freshest kid this side of the Hudson," he growled and closed the doors.

"Betcha he reports me to someone." She sounded positively gleeful. She thrived on trouble.

I was really looking forward to D.A. today. Instead of one hour, we had two on the days we cooked, eliminating our study period. Lasagna was one of my favorite dishes and I was sure Beth would follow instructions to the letter, and we'd have the best meal in the class.

"It even looks good when it's being put together," I said, cracking an egg for the cheese layer into a mixing bowl. I was good at that. My shells never ended up in the bowl.

"Yeah, I love seeing all the ingredients. It's like putting together a puzzle," Beth said. Her long hair was pinned up. Mrs. Lindsey was freaky about "Hair in the food!"

"I like jigsaw puzzles, especially the ones with five hundred pieces." It just came out. Beth and I don't discuss stuff that doesn't have something to do with cooking. But she was the one who mentioned puzzles.

"You, too? I have an E.T. puzzle. I've done it a zillion times and it never gets dull."

Now I didn't know what to say. She looked at me

expectantly. Should I tell her about my Smurf jigsaw, or the Jedi one, or the one with the skyline of New York? She probably didn't want to hear about them. So, I asked, "Is the pan ready?"

She blinked, then nodded. We didn't say much after that except that the lasagna turned out fantastic. Mrs. Lindsey sampled ours and said it was the best. Beth and I smiled at each other.

"Frannie, this is dynamite stuff. I'd be lardo, too, if someone in my house cooked this way."

"Shut up, Rachel!" Amanda ordered.

"Hey, you said you weren't talking to me."

"Now, now, children," Mrs. Lindsey said. She's fluttery and dithery about us when we're not directly involved with cooking or another project. "I think the meal was a grand success. We all want to thank Mrs. Balducci." Frannie's mother wasn't in class, but everyone applauded (and Rachel put her fingers in her mouth and whistled). Frannie smiled. Her dimples have dimples.

"Next week, it's . . . let's see . . ." Mrs. Lindsey put on her granny glasses and checked out her Rolodex. She's one of the few teachers who doesn't have a computer. "Here it is. It's Cory's turn to bring in a dish from Mrs. Matthewson."

My face was already reddening when Rachel said,

"Mrs. Matthewson doesn't live with Cory."

"Oh, dear. I am sorry, Cory. I didn't realize."

"That's okay," I whispered.

How could Rachel do this to me? I know somewhere deep down inside, where her mouth doesn't function, that she thinks she's being helpful. But I wanted to die. Especially when Tommy called out, "Maybe Mr. Delancey will give her a recipe. She's nuts about him!" And everyone snickered.

"What does Mr. Delancey have to do with this?" The teacher was waving her fingers in the air and shaking her small head in amazement. I had to put an end to this. "Mrs. Lindsey, I'll have a recipe next week. Don't worry about it."

"All right, Cory. If you say so, I won't fret."

But I would.

Chapter 4

Mrs. Winchell is always astounded by the fact that I can bunt right down the first base line. "Cory, you're a little package of TNT!"

Compliments make me terribly uncomfortable except when they're about baseball. I know I'm good. The whole team does. Baseball is the only time I feel I'm a part of Markham. It's nice while it lasts.

I watched Binky Holifax. He wears eyeglasses so thick that the lenses remind me of the bottoms of Coke bottles. When he runs, which is rare, since he usually strikes out, his helmet topples from his bushy Afro. But Binky *knows* baseball better than anyone on the Eagles. He fairly breathes the game. He'd give me the steal sign at the perfect moment. He'll make a great major league manager someday. He rubbed his stomach and pinched his chin and I was off with the pitch. The catcher never got the ball out of her glove.

It was only a practice but the kids gave me a huge cheer. Tommy, who was playing second, shook his head. "You're something else, Cory. I think you could beat my dog at running." From Tommy, that's a *big* compliment.

"Way to go, kiddo! Shake 'em up!" Rachel's megaphone-enhanced voice reached me. She is wild about megaphones. She doesn't know anything about the game except for bunt and steal. She says since those are my specialties, and since I'm the reason she comes to see the Eagles, they're all she has to remember. Whenever I'm not up or on base, she reads the *National Nosybody*.

The practice lasted another thirty minutes. I bunted twice more, stole second and third, and flew out to the center fielder, who dropped the ball, and that allowed me to circle the bases. A fine afternoon.

"You have a good balance. You'll be great with kites," Rachel announced, jumping down from the small stands.

"You need good balance for kite flying?"

Rachel snorted. "Sure you do. Someone has to hold the reel properly."

"I thought reels were for fishing."

"I got my work cut out for me. Don't worry, kiddo. We'll have the best kite in the contest."

Mrs. Winchell had an appointment at the hair-dresser so she wasn't driving the team home. I knew that last night and had told Daddy. I didn't mention kites, though. Suddenly, I stopped short. "What contest?"

"Didn't I tell you about it?"

"You know very well you didn't"

"Well, I didn't want you to get all bent out of shape. You do that when there's something important happening."

"I do?"

"Sure, like when Loony Lindsey said it was your turn to bring in a recipe. I thought you'd melt into the oven. Have to learn to take things in stride, kiddo. You could die of an early heart attack if you don't. I read that in the *Nosybody* today." She waved a copy.

"Rachel, would you please tell me about the kite contest *now*. Is it for school?

"No way! Port Hudson runs it. The Chamber of Commerce or one of those dumb, stuffy adult things. It's over the Memorial Day weekend."

"I don't know if I can help then. My mother has custody of me on some holidays." I couldn't keep track of which.

"You have to help me."

I looked at Rachel. She seemed helpless—her pasty

skin was smeared from *Nosybody* newsprint and her blazer was wrecked. She'd used it as a pennant during practice and had whacked Mrs. Holifax in the face with it. (The woman's screams were the loudest from the stands all afternoon.) Mrs. Holifax's walnut-colored makeup dotted the Markham golden crest.

"I promise."

"You won't be sorry, kiddo. We're going to win." And for emphasis, she punched me in the arm.

I could just imagine the way Rachel would react if we did win. She'd hoot and holler and hop around like those maniac contestants on game shows. Rachel loved those programs. I'd never act like that.

After dinner, I begged Dad to let Rachel come over after school. "We won't get the place too messed up."

"Cory, I trust you. It's Rachel," he said frankly. "Remember the time she came over to make decorations for the Christmas pageant? I was here then. In my room, but still in the apartment. When I strolled into the living room, there was glue slathered on the TV screen and on the ceiling. The set I understand. The ceiling?"

"Rachel just wanted to see how the decorations would look hanging. The glue wasn't dry yet and that's when the decoration and the wet glue hit the screen."

He laughed and tugged on his wispy sideburns. "Okay, to prove I'm not an ogre, you can work on the kite here. In your bedroom, however."

"Got it."

"Good," and he turned his attention to the tube, where M*A*S*H, his all-time favorite show, was being rerun for the umpteenth time.

"There's one more thing, Daddy." He gave a long, drawn-out groan. I giggled. "It's no big deal. Well, it's kind of a deal. It's my turn to hand in a recipe for Domestic Arrangements. I need one next week. And we don't have a microwave in the classroom."

"Even with one, pumpkin, I'm hardly Julia Child. Why don't you call your mother?"

"Mom isn't the French Chef, either." When Daddy was on the road, Mom and I ate out a lot. So much so that I knew every restaurant on the West Side of Manhattan from sushi bars to family-owned Greek restaurants, where the owners always wanted to fatten me and Mom up.

"I realize that, but she has friends who cook. I'm sure she can come up with something."

While Dad watched M*A*S*H, I called Mom. She was delighted to hear from me. She likes me more now that she doesn't see me on a daily basis.

"I'm sure Serita can come up with something. The woman is not only the most efficient assistant in the world, she is also the best cook."

"Mom, nothing real fancy."

"Oh, Cory, don't be such a spoilsport. Wouldn't a simply outrageous dish make a huge splash with your classmates?"

I considered. "Maybe. But I don't want to take any chances. I don't want to get laughed out of the sixth grade."

"My little fraidy cat!" Mom laughed. "Well, at least you have that awful child, Rachel, to protect you. She does do some good."

"Rachel is my best friend."

"She is your *only* friend, Cory. You should cultivate other friendships."

Rachel is one of the few things my parents agree about. "They don't cultivate me," I said flatly.

Mom stayed silent for a moment then spoke in a soft voice. I could just see her long, amber-colored page-boy, and her round blue eyes blinking rapidly. "I'm sorry, Cory. I shouldn't have come on so strong. But you know how I feel about that child."

"Yes."

"Don't worry, though, You'll probably emerge as

the most popular kid in the seventh grade. Wait till next year, as they say in sports, right?"

"Yes."

"Cory, there's another reason I'm so happy that you called. Guess what fashion designer has box seats for the Yankees this weekend?"

I let out a shriek. Dad came running. I was bouncing up and down so he knew Mom had said something to please me. And that pleased him.

He let me go over to Rachel's apartment after talking to Mom. "But not too long," he warned.

I think he really believes if I hang out with Rachel too much, she'll influence me in some evil way. It hasn't happened since October, why should it happen now?

As soon as I reached the Vellarses' door, the poodles yapped. They belonged to The Fourth Mrs. Vellars. She answered the door. The apricot-colored toy dogs nipped at her spike-heeled slippers. She's tall and bony and looks like a high fashion model. Physically, except for the tall part, she reminds me of my mother, but that's where the resemblance stops. My mom wasn't cut out for raising a kid and she eventually admitted defeat. The Fourth Mrs. Vellars would never concede. She's as phony as her put-on British accent.

"Is Rachel expecting you?"

She always asks me that. I always reply, "Yes," because that's what she wants to hear. She's the kind of person you just don't drop in on. I think she has an appointment book for brushing her teeth.

I hurried through the overly decorated apartment and up the stair to Rachel's room. I paused before entering. The inside of Rachel's room is always a shock. A nuclear meltdown couldn't destroy the place better. There are clothes, clean and dirty, in one pile, to the right of the door, and her massive collection of *National Nosybodys* and *Teen Screen Fanzines* to the left. Once you walk the narrow path into the center of the large room, you get to a chair that is also covered with clothes and tapes. Rachel is in the middle of the four poster, headphones on. I walked to the front of her bed and crunched a bag of potato chips under my feet.

"I'm here!" I announced loudly, standing right in front of her.

She tapped the headphones. "Rolling Stones." I nodded and sat down carefully on another chair. It didn't have anything on it but it wobbled. Rachel is on a Stones kick. Two weeks ago, it was the Whistle Blues Bus, the biggest new wave group around. Two weeks from now, it might be Dolly Parton.

The song must have ended in a few seconds because she yanked off the headphones. "Wow! Do I ever have something to tell you!"

"Me first." And I told her we could do the kite and she was pleased. She punched me in the forearm.

"All right! Your old man's not so bad."

"I know. What's so big—"

"I was looking out the window—"

"With your binoculars?" I asked. Rachel has a set of opera glasses left by The Third Mrs. Vellars, who sang with the chorus of the Metropolitan Opera.

"Naturally, how else could I get a clear view of the street? You're dense sometimes, kiddo. Anyway, who comes out of the Kingsley but Beth and her old lady. Beth was crying and her mother didn't look too thrilled, either."

I thought back to how nice Beth had been in D.A. today, talking about the puzzles. I didn't mention that to Rachel; Rachel doesn't like it when I have real conversations with most people. She doesn't object if I talk to Tommy or Binky or Jenny Chee, who's nine-and-a-half and in the sixth grade because she's a genius.

"Then Mr. Lowery zoomed out of the underground parking lot. I know his Volvo," she added. "I tried to zero in on his face but the lighting was lousy. I don't think he was happy, though. He's the type to be sad if his wife and kids are. My old man isn't like that. My old man isn't like most fathers," she ended with a sigh. Then she shrugged, as if getting rid of a sudden chill. "Aren't you dying to know what upset Little Miss Sunshine, kiddo?"

Okay, I was curious, but not in Rachel's ghoulish way. Yet if I said I wasn't, she'd pout and rant, "Kiddo, you're so dumb about real people. Why don't you read the *National Nosybody* instead of all those dumb books you're always reading?" She said similar stuff on other occasions and I didn't want this one spoiled. I was too excited about Dad letting us work on the kite and about Mom taking me to a Yankee game to get Rachel upset with me.

"Yeah, I guess so. But I don't have much chance of finding out why Beth was crying."

Wrong.

Chapter 5

Beth wasn't on the bus the next morning. Amanda and Frannie were awfully quiet. Rachel babbled on about the kite, its bridles, the decorations we'd put on, and something called dowel sticks. I considered buying disaster insurance for my room.

Beth showed up during study period. She wasn't in the hushed room for more than two minutes when she got up and spoke to Mr. Pell then disappeared. I wondered about it for a second (because of what Rachel had told me last night) then went back to reading a biography of Tracy Austin. I finished a chapter and glanced at the wall clock. Another ten minutes left to the period; I was tired of reading. And just sitting in class, staring off into space isn't much fun. Rachel was on the other side of the room so we couldn't pass notes back and forth. She doesn't like notes, anyhow; Rachel likes to talk. I asked Mr. Pell for a bathroom pass. He readily gave it to me. That's one of the neat things about Markham. You can get a pass to anywhere at anytime. You also don't have to be afraid of getting your lunch money stolen in the bathroom the way it was at P.S. 599. That never happened to me, but it happened to Inez.

The bathroom at Markham doesn't look like a school john, either. It had incredibly high ceilings, a chandelier, three huge stalls each with its own little sink, a big communal sink, and even a claw-footed bathtub. Mrs. Albert, who filled us in on the history of the school as well as teaching us about Russian tsars, said bootleggers (people who smuggled illegal liquor during Prohibition) actually made gin in that same bathtub. I'd never wash myself in it.

I wanted to sit on one of the lavender-colored chairs and think. I can do that by myself but not in a crowded study hall. But one of the two chairs was already occupied—by Beth. She was sobbing. Uh-oh, when I hear someone cry, I get all weepy.

Suddenly, she jerked her head up. Tears streaked her perfectly shaped face. "Oh, Cory, I'm—I'm glad it's you."

She was? I sat on the opposite chair. There was a small vanity table between us. A hand-printed sign over it reads, "Please comb hair here. Not over little sinks, big sink, or giant tub. Thank you." It was a truly remarkable sign; there wasn't any graffiti on it.

"I'm sorry you're crying, Beth," I said, hoping that the sound of my voice would halt my tears.

"Cory, it was horrible! Hor—rible. Why'd I have to come to school today?"

Rachel said Beth had been crying last night, too. Whatever upset her was *big*. I was kind of scared, but I kept talking, "I guess your parents wanted you to come." Which was a dumb thing to say but the only thing I could think of at the moment.

Obviously, Beth thought it was the perfect comment. "They did, Cory. They—they said it'd be too much for me to stay home. Too many memories."

Uh-oh. Someone died. I could tell.

"Fluffy's dead!" she wailed. "We had him put to sleep. It was ho—horrible." Tears gushed down her cheeks and mine as well. Fluffy was a pet. I knew about pets dying. My tears were for Gilligan, the old tom we had back in Manhattan.

"I'm sorry, Beth. I—I had a cat once."

"There's no cat like Fluffy," she sniffled.

Then we both cried without saying anything. My cries subsided first, and although my voice was gulpy, I spoke. "Whatever made the vet put Fluffy to sleep, I'm very, very sorry. I love cats a whole lot."

"She had feline leukemia. That's a terrible disease," she added through her sobs. "The vet said he had to do it. Why, Cory?" She wiped her nose. "I would have given her lots and lots of love. Wouldn't that have helped?"

I knew that illness was incurable. The vet had probably told Beth that. No use in repeating information she had already heard. Instead, I looked down at my pleated skirt and said, "Sometimes really lousy things happen. When I lived in the city, when my whole family lived together, we had a cat. He was super. Anyhow, it was a hot summer night. My parents had argued all through supper at this French bistro . . ." Why was I telling Beth all this? Because it seemed perfectly natural. I continued, "And we came home. It was real stuffy in the apartment. We lived on the fourth floor. We threw open the windows. No one saw Gilligan. He must've been hot and stuffy, too, because he took one look at an open window and leaped out." My voice broke at this point. Beth grabbed my hand and squeezed it. "He was alive when we got downstairs, but when we got to the vet, the vet said Gilligan was too old to get through an operation so we had to . . . had to . . ." And I squeezed Beth's hand.

We sat like that, crying and nodding, for the rest of the period. The bell chimed softly. "We'd better get going. I mean, I'd better get going." Now that all the crying was over, I felt somehow better. I'd told Rachel about Gilligan but just that he'd died, not the whole story. It was good to get it out.

"You still miss him, don't you?"

"Yes, more than I realized. The apartment wouldn't be so empty when I get home."

"Daddy said I could get two cats tomorrow, but they wouldn't replace Fluffy. No one will!" she added fiercely.

"No, but maybe you can love another one for just being itself."

The second bell sounded. Another neat thing about Markham is that no teacher, except Mrs. Grinwold, who teaches math, gets too upset if you're late for the class. We had art next and Mr. Cornelius barely takes attendance; he's too enthused about slapping paints on canvas or smushing clay together. The door opened and two first-grader types made mad dashes for the stalls. They ignored us completely.

"Do you want me to tell Mr. Cornelius that you're sick or something?" I asked, after splashing cold water on my face. I dried it with scratchy paper towels. Those towels are the same everywhere.

"Thanks for listening, Cory. I mean it. If Mr. Cornelius notices I'm not there, tell him I'm sick. But I don't need the nurse!" Our art teacher gets more dithery than Mrs. Lindsey when a kid cuts herself or throws up in class.

"Are you sure you don't want me to stay with you?"

She blinked. "No. You've been a big help, Cory. I'm really glad you were the one who came in. And I'm sorry about Gilligan. Bet he was a terrific friend."

"He was. I'm sorry about Fluffy, too. See you, Beth."

"See you, Cory."

My first *real* conversation with another kid. We had something in common, even if it was something sad. Even though I hadn't felt bad before I spoke with Beth, and then I felt rotten when I was talking to her (but a little good, too), I felt better now. It was crazy! I practically skipped to art.

49

Chapter 6

The good feeling lasted until lunch when Rachel pointed to Beth, who was flanked by Amanda and Frannie, and said, "What's going on with her? Remember I said she was bawling last night? Then she came into school late and then disappeared during study hall." Rachel never missed anything. "I'm going to find out what's going on."

I tugged at her sleeve. "Don't go over there. I know what's bothering Beth."

"*You* do?"

"I went to the bathroom during study—"

"Yeah, saw that, too."

"Right, and Beth was in there. She was crying. Her cat died."

"Aw, her dumb cat died? And here I was, thinking it was something important." Rachel chomped on her egg salad sandwich.

"Cats are not dumb," I said defensively. "I had one. I told you that."

She swallowed hard. "Yeah, you did. Okay, *your* cat probably wasn't stupid."

"And I cried when it died."

She gave an exaggerated sigh. "Yeah, you would. And so would Beth." *Would Rachel?* "I dunno, maybe cats are different from dogs. We never had any cats. I sure wish someone would do something to her stinking 'poodies,' though."

"Your stepmother would be very upset."

Rachel hooted and people turned our way. I nibbled on my peanut butter and raisin sandwich. "Nothing rattles The Fourth Mrs. Vellars. Except me," Rachel added with a huge grin.

She stayed put and never said anything to Beth. I was relieved about that. Not that Beth had told me her story in confidence, but if Rachel bounded over with the news, Beth would immediately know that I'd blabbed the whole thing. And I really wasn't a big mouth. Probably because I never had anything interesting to tell anyone.

That evening, Dad helped me pack. He's always afraid I'll forget something important like a toothbrush or my sneakers. He doesn't realize that those are the first items I cram into my suitcase. Or that maybe, just maybe, Mom, who lives right smack in the middle of New York City, could get me those things if they weren't in my overnight bag.

"Daddy, can we get another cat?"

He sat on the edge of my bed and rubbed his moustache. "I don't see why not."

"We can? Oh, wow!" And I gave him a great big hug.

"Did you think I'd say no?"

I sat next to him and said, "You never mentioned Gilligan much after it happened. I wasn't sure how you felt."

"And I wasn't sure how you felt. I didn't know if you wanted another cat so soon or were still grieving for Gilligan. Have you wanted one for a long time?"

"Well, I've been thinking about Gilligan, but I didn't know how much I wanted another cat until today." And I filled him in on Beth's cat.

"I'm glad she had you to talk to. You obviously helped her through a difficult time. I'm proud of you."

Daddy and I talked about where to get a cat and we decided on an animal shelter. He said we could go next week. We were discussing whether to get a kitten or a grown cat when the intercom sounded.

Mom had arrived.

She waltzed into the apartment a minute later. She

looked gorgeous, as usual, with her long amber hair swept in to a French knot and her ivory-shaded makeup expertly applied. She wore a beige linen pant-suit and red blouse, both her own creations. Virginia Matthewson Creations, Inc., was a big name in the fashion world for the working woman. Especially for the petite ones. Mom is tiny.

"All packed?" she asked. She gets nervous around Daddy after a few minutes of small talk. He feels the same way.

"Toothbrush and sneakers."

"I do hope you're bringing more than that, Cory!" Mom said, taking me seriously, as usual. "We're going out to dinner after the game and out for Sunday brunch. You packed something suitable, I hope?"

"Sorry, but her Oscar de la Rentas are all in storage," Dad said. He meant it as a joke. Oscar de la Renta is this real fancy fashion designer. Mom loves his stuff and tried to do similar designs when she was starting out. Until she found out that her talents were in clothes for the office.

Mom gave a quick shake of her head. That meant she didn't appreciate his joke and that her temper was growing short.

"I packed the paisley jumper and the ruffled yellow blouse," I said. They were scaled-down VMC styles.

Mom relaxed slightly. She said, "I'll have her back by seven o'clock on Sunday evening. Is that okay, Jim?"

"No problem, Virginia. Have fun, Cory. Hope the Yanks win it for you."

I was happy when we stepped into the outer hall and pushed for the elevator. Happy until the door at the far end of the corridor opened and out popped Rachel. She was wearing a multistained T-shirt, ripped jeans, and no shoes. Her feet were multistained, too. I think she was working on her kite or some sort of sticky project. Either that or she had a jelly-making factory hidden in the duplex.

Mom didn't groan but her mouth set in this tight little line, the kind she used to get right before she'd have a big battle with Daddy. Mom, please don't set Rachel off. I won't be around all weekend. It'll be lonely for her. Her parents are going to the mountains. They're leaving her with the housekeeper, who's so terrified of Rachel that Rachel doesn't have any fun tormenting her. I hoped Mrs. Heffernan would be around. Rachel liked to play gin rummy with her.

"Neat outfit, Mrs. Matthewson," she said by way of a greeting. "I'm into originals myself." And she pointed to her messy clothes and howled. Mom grimaced.

54

"So, what are you going to do this weekend?" I asked quickly.

"This and that. I'll find something. I always do. Too bad you won't be around, kiddo. With the old man and The Fourth Mrs. Vellars away, we could've *really* had good times. Full run of the place with dippy Gwendolyn too scared to lift a fat finger."

The elevator arrived. I said good-bye to Rachel. When the doors closed, Mom glanced down at me. "Cory, can't you find any other friends? I can't believe it. That girl is impossible. You can't honestly tell me you *like* her."

"I honestly like her."

Mom gave that toss of her head again. "You'll see, Cory. Mark my words. You'll see someday that she's not the right sort of friend for you."

What a way to start a weekend.

Chapter 7

The first thing Mom and I did on Saturday morning was travel down to her showroom on Fashion Avenue. That's what the street sign reads. Actually, it's Seventh Avenue. But at this location, there's so much business in fashion that someone, a mayor, I guess, decided to rename the street. I think that's confusing for tourists.

Mom's offices are on the twenty-third floor of this weird-shaped building. The building has more corridors and twists and turns than a haunted house. Mom's double doors are smoky glass and the VMC insignia is written in frosted white swirls.

Business has been great lately, which is why she's launching a new line. She told me about it over Chinese takeout last night. She'll be doing frilly dresses and some floor length skirts for evening wear. "Not

Oscar de La Renta stuff," she assured me. "Just Virginia Matthewson pretty." She was all excited about the new line. When she's enthused, she bites her lip and doesn't mind getting lipstick on her teeth, and she giggles. We both do. I love Mom best when she's excited about her work.

We entered the showroom, which was busy, even on a Saturday. That's how good business was. Mom said my scaled-down versions of her creations would be waiting for me. I'd be getting the fall line. When we lived in Manhattan, I wore the outfits often since we went out to eat a lot. But in Port Hudson, I don't have much of a chance to wear her neat clothes. It bothered me sometimes that I couldn't show off Mom's super fashions. They looked lonely in my closet—as lonely as I felt staring at them.

Mom's assistant and best friend is Serita. I have no idea what her last name is. She's over six feet tall, with long, straight ebony hair, olive skin, and laughing brown eyes that are partially hidden by enormous glasses. She's kind of overwhelming but she likes me.

"Cory, how you doing? Since you moved to the boonies, we haven't seen you nearly enough." She planted a sloppy kiss on my cheek.

"Hi, Serita. I'm fine. Mom's giving me the fall line

today. I can hardly wait."

"I considered sending the whole thing up," Mom said, "but I know how much you enjoy coming to the showroom."

Did I ever! I glanced around the reception area. It's a beautiful space, all done in greens and beiges, with dark coral accents. This area showed up VMC in its best light. Oh, Mom's small office was the same, but the rest of the offices, Serita's included, were a total and complete mess. Serita called them "Artistic Chaos." I called them "Rachel's room transplanted to the Big Apple."

I went into the back and phones were ringing off the hooks. Order takers yelled. A seamstress worked frantically on a skirt. It was a wild scene. Mom built this company from nothing three years ago. Before that, she worked from the house and assisted a sportswear designer. When he retired, she leased these offices, with financial help from friends and a little from Daddy, and she drove herself to make Virginia Matthewson Creations a hit. Of course, all her work made her even more abstracted with me. But it was okay. I already knew the business was more important to her than I was. I gave up crying about it in the fourth grade.

Seeing the office crazy with activity and Mom's beaming face made me happy. I was so proud of her! I squeezed her hand. She smiled.

By the time I'd oohed and ahhed over all the beautiful outfits, it was time to get to Yankee Stadium. There were three huge boxes of clothes.

"Are you two going to schlepp these up to the Bronx?" Serita asked.

Mom, who'd been bright and exuberant while showing me the creations, suddenly looked downcast. "I hadn't thought about that part of it," she admitted.

"No problem," Serita said cheerfully. "I'll drop them by your apartment when we close up."

"How could I have forgotten that detail?" Mom said, when we were back on the street again, walking over to Madison Avenue, where we'd catch the express bus to the Bronx. She uses rental cars to pick me up in the suburbs, but she refuses to drive around in the city. I don't blame her. "Another one of our visits getting off on the wrong foot. Think I'll ever get it right, Cory?" She heaved a sigh.

"Nothing's wrong." Mom tends to get worried when the least little thing gets turned around. I inherited that trait from her. "You know, it's like in Domestic Arrangements when I wanted to put the lasagna in

the oven before putting on the mozzarella topping. Good thing Beth was my partner. She notices stuff like that."

"Beth? Not Rachel?"

"No, Beth Lowery."

"How nice!"

Now, we were getting close to a subject that could get us into a big hassle—about Rachel being my only friend. Yet I wanted to tell Mom about getting another cat, and the only way I could do that was to tell her about my chat with Beth. Which I did, during the ride. Mom was properly sympathetic about Fluffy and pleased by the way I'd comforted Beth.

"You're a very special child, Cory. Even someone who's as dense as I am about kids can see that. I am a bit surprised that Jim didn't bring up getting another cat earlier. He's usually on top of your feelings."

"Mom, I didn't know I wanted a cat until the other day. Besides, Daddy's not a mind reader."

"I suppose," she murmured.

I hated talking about Daddy to Mom or vice versa. They don't like each other, but I love them both. In different ways, but I do love them. I looked out the window.

The game was dynamite, with the Yanks coming from behind in the bottom of the ninth with three runs to win nine-to-seven. And Ricky Henderson, of the Oakland A's, stole two bases. He's the best. I whooped and hollered. Mom laughed and cheered, too. She let me eat three franks, several Cokes, a bag of popcorn, and two ice creams. She went hysterical when I asked where we were going for dinner.

"I've gained five pounds just watching you," she teased.

Later, we ate in a French bistro near the apartment. I fell asleep as soon as we returned. The next morning, Mom read *The Times* while I read a book she bought for me. She buys stacks of mysteries and biographies for my visits. I like the quiet time when we're reading.

Our next stop was Sunday brunch. That's a tradition in our family. Daddy and I even keep to it in Port Hudson. We don't go out, though. We just whip up some eggs and sausages and, if we're real adventurous, home fries. It's the one time when we don't use the microwave. Mom loves to go out, though. So do I. She hadn't decided on which restaurant. The one we used to like had turned into a video arcade since I last visited.

We stepped out of the creaky elevator and who should I spot immediately but Inez Flores! I practically leaped into the air. "Hi, Inez, how's old P.S. 599?"

She'd grown at least two inches since I'd last seen her, over Thanksgiving. She looked awfully mature. Bet she wore a bra and not the training kind, either.

She didn't say anything right away. Good grief, as Charlie Brown would say. She doesn't recognize me. How could that be? We were best friends less than a year ago and she knew me back in November. We talked then. Now she looked at me like I was E.T.'s worst enemy.

I gulped. "It's me, Cory Matthewson."

"I know it's you, Cory," she said awkwardly.

I peered into the dim lobby. There was a girl behind her, not Ginny McNeil. Someone I didn't know.

"Who is she?" the girl demanded.

"Cory. We used to go to school together. She doesn't live here anymore."

The girl pushed past Inez and stood in the elevator. "C'mon, Inez," she said impatiently. "She doesn't live here anymore. She doesn't count."

Inez blinked, gave me a little shrug and said, while the elevator doors were closing, "See you, Cory."

I couldn't believe what had happened. What kind of an awful person was Inez hanging out with? "I'd never, ever do that," I said fiercely.

"Do what? I think the Lime Banana is a good place. It's not a singles hangout. Giorgio told me about it. He takes his family there a lot." Giorgio is her accountant.

When I didn't say anything, Mom repeated, "Do what?"

"Be so rude to an old friend. And old *best* friend at that. Just because that new girl didn't want Inez to talk to me. Why'd Inez listen to her, huh?" My bottom lip quivered.

"Cory, even in this atrocious lighting, I can tell you're going to cry. Please don't. Just tell me what happened, okay?" Mom hates scenes.

I told her quickly. "I'd never do that to someone," I added.

"Of course not. That's what makes you special, Cory. Distance has made me painfully aware of that," Mom said softly, touching my hair.

I sniffled, determined not to cry. "We're closer now, Mom. And we're having a good weekend, too."

"Thanks, Cory." She hugged me. "Off to the Lime Banana!"

Dad got a kick out of the boxes we dragged in on Sunday night. Mom left quickly but kissed me several times. Maybe she was beginning to see me as a person and not just as a kid.

"Want to see all my great stuff?" I pointed to the

boxes. "I'd better hang up all the clothes before they get wrinkled."

"You do that. I'll, um, look at the clothes later, okay?"

I giggled; he grinned. Daddy isn't much for fashion. "Listen, you had some phone calls."

"Rachel knew I'd be away until tonight," I said, picking out a mohair suit and putting it on a hanger.

"Rachel called a few minutes before you came in. But Beth called yesterday."

The suit dropped to the floor. The hanger clattered as it hit the leg of my desk. "Beth called?"

"Isn't she the girl with the cat?" I nodded. "I told her you wouldn't be home until this evening. She made a point of giving me her number. It's unlisted."

Ours wasn't but no one ever called. Except for Rachel. Even though she lived down the hall, she liked to use the phone. I was the only person who called her, too.

Daddy handed me Beth's number. I made the call on the kitchen phone. Daddy disappeared into the living room. "Hello, may I speak to Beth, please?" My voice cracked on every word.

"This is Beth. Who's this?"

"Cory, Cory Ma—"

"Hi, hi, I'm so glad you called. I didn't recognize your voice. Your father said you were in New York with your mother. Did you have fun?"

"Yes, it was a good visit."

"Visit? Ooops, I'm sorry, Cory. I remember, your folks are divorced."

"Nothing to be sorry about," I said easily. "I'm used to it. I like visiting Mom. I love living with Dad."

"You really know how to put things, Cory. Like when you helped me about . . . Fluffy." Pain crept into her voice. I decided against telling her I was getting a new cat. Maybe another time. "You were really understanding. Thanks."

"I was just there."

"More than that. But listen, I didn't just want to thank you. I want you to come over to my apartment Tuesday."

I stared at the white phone in disbelief.

"Cory, are you still there?"

"I'm here. Tuesday is—" I was ready to say great when I remembered. "I have a game Tuesday."

"Okay, Wednesday then. Tomorrow's out because I have a violin lesson."

"You play the violin?"

"My instructor doesn't think so!" We laughed. "I

really wish I could play better. You know, the way Frannie is with the piano."

"Yes, she's good." Frannie, who seemed more afraid of people than me, actually gave performances at various assemblies. She'd get deathly pale before sitting on the piano bench. Then when her fingers touched the keys, color would return to her face, and I could tell she was enjoying herself.

"So, is Wednesday okay?"

"Terrific."

I couldn't believe it! I was invited to Beth's. Would Daddy let me go? Oh, he had to. I rushed into the living room where he was working on the computer. "Excuse me," I said politely. Daddy is pretty even-tempered but he gets angry when he's annoyed at the machine. I sure didn't want him annoyed right now. He held up one hand to me and studied the monitor. A couple of minutes passed but they seemed like six hours.

"Okay, that program is complete." He rubbed his beard. "Now, what can I do for—"

"You have to let me! You just have to!" The words spilled out of me. Quickly, I told him. "It's the first time I've been invited to someone else's house. Except for Rachel's."

"Mmmm, well, let's see," his eyes twinkled. "I think it can be arranged. The Kingsley is next door. Yeah, you can go."

I giggled, hugged him, giggled again, and ran into my room. What a super weekend! I flopped on the bed, thinking the happiest of thoughts. And I didn't call Rachel.

Chapter 8

"All this week, we work on the kite, kiddo. We're gonna have the best box kite around."

I was about to ask Rachel what a box kite was when the beginning of her sentence hit me. All this week . . . "Rachel, um, I can't work on the kite tomorrow. Baseball."

She wrinkled her nose. "Oh, heck. Four days out of five then."

"Not Wednesday, either."

The bus had pulled in. Clem glowered at Rachel, tipped his cap to me when I said good morning, and we slipped into our seats. Beth hadn't been waiting at the stop. Amanda and Frannie weren't in the bus. From my eavesdropping, I learned that sometimes Amanda's father drove all of them to Markham. So, I wasn't in any imminent danger of having Beth dash over and say, "Don't forget about Wednesday, Cory.

You're coming over to my apartment."

"Why can't we work on it then? We've got lots and lots of stuff to do, kiddo. I have all the equipment. Drove Mrs. Heffernan nuts over the weekend picking all my gear out of storage. She grumbled that I'd better win this year 'cause she's sick of storing the junk. I told her not to worry. This time, I have a partner. Hey, are you listening?"

"Oh, sure, Rachel. Heard every word. But I can't make it Wednesday." Shutting my eyes, I spoke rapidly, "I'm going over to Beth's."

"You're *what?*" she shrieked.

I cowered in my seat. "You heard me."

"Yeah, but I still don't believe it. You're kidding, right?"

"No, she invited me."

"I bet she did. Yeah, because of that cat business. It's just an excuse, you know, kiddo. *They're* going to study you, dissect you, like a lab experiment."

My pulse quickened. I gazed at Rachel out of the corner of my eye. Her face was set in its earnest position, which means she wasn't moving a muscle. Not for a good five seconds. Then she exploded.

"You're not that innocent, are you, kiddo?" She shook her head. "Bouncy Bethie isn't inviting you over without a deep, dark, ulterior motive. The rest of the snobbie-creepos will be there. They're going to turn you inside out, demanding that you answer their probing questions. It'll be like Chinese water torture. Or the rack. Or worse!"

"But Beth didn't mention the others—"

"They travel in a pack, like wolves. Remember the article I told you about, the one in the *Nosybody*, about the guy who lived with wolves then got eaten by his pack?"

I hoped my Cheerios and buttered toast breakfast didn't land up on the seats. I have a nervous stomach when I'm upset. "Rachel, they're not going to eat me alive. Besides, how do you know what they'll do if they do show up? Did they put *you* under the hot lights?"

She laughed as the bus reached school. "Me? Are you putting me on, kiddo? I wouldn't be caught dead. I'm too smart for them. Nah, I heard about their tactics. Ask Jenny Chee. She'll tell you. They did it to her." She must have caught the disbelieving expression on my face because she hollered, "Hey, Jenny! C'mere!"

"Can't you wait to hoot and holler? Like when you're off my bus?" Clem demanded.

She ignored him and grabbed Jenny's doll-like arm as she walked down the aisle. Jenny's beautiful almond eyes widened. "What do you wish, Rachel?" she asked softly.

"Let's get off the bus," I suggested lightly.

"Nah, let old Clem wait a second. It's not like he's on a *real* schedule. Jenny, you tell Cory here about the time Amanda invited you over to her house."

Jenny glanced down at her green loafers, then she looked up at me. "There is not much to tell."

"Like fish!" Rachel said. "Jenny's old man and mine travel on the same train and her old man told mine that the snobbie-creepos really gave her a hard time. C'mon, Jenny, tell it like it is."

"Jenny, you don't have to say anything," I said kindly. She spoke to me once in awhile and she was sweet, even if she was a little kid.

"It is all right, Cory," she said, probably knowing that Rachel wouldn't let her off the hook. "At the beginning of the term, in September, Amanda invited me over to her home. Frannie, Beth, and Maria—"

"Maria moved away a couple of days before you moved in, kiddo. Consider yourself real lucky."

"I hope this ain't one of them long senate-type speeches," Clem said from the front of the bus. Everyone else had gotten off.

Jenny continued in her evenly spaced tones. "They seemed to be nice enough. But they asked many ques-

71

tions. Impolite questions. I could not answer such private matters. I told them so. They stopped being so nice. It was an unhappy experience." And at the memory of the unhappiness, Jenny's eyes welled with tears. She murmured, "Excuse me, please." And she scurried down the aisle and into the street.

"Hallelujah! One down, two to go. You two kids are leaving, aren't you?" Clem asked.

"Yeah, we got our business done. You can move this heap now," Rachel said, bounding out.

I didn't scurry or bound. I walked slowly, said good-bye to Clem, who muttered something in reply, and followed Rachel into the street.

"See? I told you, kiddo. They're gonna make you into a lab experiment. I wouldn't be surprised if they're doing something about behavior jazz for their June science project. Hey, say something, kiddo. You heard what the little kid said. She wouldn't lie."

"Rachel, she was in tears."

"Yeah, well, what they did to her was pretty heavy. Believe you me, kiddo, I wouldn't take it—"

"Then why did you have to be so mean to Jenny? Ooooh, Rachel Vellars, how could you?"

Chapter 9

How could Rachel be so unfeeling? Couldn't she see how hurt Jenny was? Or how scared I was? What were the girls going to do to me? Put me under a microscope? Ask about my parents? Did I have my period yet? Oh, wow. I didn't want to go through with this. Beth spoke to me nicely during D.A. but didn't mention Wednesday. Maybe she'd forgotten about it? Then I could just not show up. But I wanted to and I didn't really think she'd forgotten.

Rachel didn't read my anger. She was her jolly, noisy self during lunch and for the rest of the day. She came over that afternoon, armed with sticks, newspaper—"You'd be shocked at the amount of newspaper people in this building toss out. Mrs. Heffernan gave me all this stuff."—scissors, paste, tape, and even a small saw. "Don't worry. I'm terrific with this kiddo.

Use it every year. Haven't lost a limb yet!" she hooted.

Then she lectured me on kite flying. "It's an art, you see. You have to watch the wind and know just when to let your kite go. Stick with me, kiddo. We are going to win this contest. I've come close before, but this time, I'm going to win that big cup. No one to stop me," she added fiercely.

"You've entered the contest before?" And who was she so angry with?

"Yeah. You surprised?"

"A little. You never enter anything in school. Or join anything, either."

"Every contest Markham has is dumb. The parents get all involved. Like the science project. The parents have to come see the exhibits. You'll see. That happens in June. It's a crock. The old folks aren't really interested. My old man wouldn't be. And The Fourth Mrs. Vellars breaks out in hives if there are more than two kids in a room." She scratched her face. "Um . . ."

I could tell she was embarrassed. Rachel didn't like talking, *really* talking about her family. "And I know you hate sports."

"Kite flying isn't a sport like baseball. It's different. I dunno. It's like when I'm out there, I'm not me, but

74

that kite dancing in the sky. I feel free," she said dreamily.

"Like when I take off to steal a base. I promise I'll help you with the kite, Rachel," I said thoughtfully. "You said you came close to winning but—"

"No buts this year, kiddo. Monkey-faced Maria is long gone. She beat me out. Snobbie-creepo. Someone helped her with her kite. An adult. That's cheating. I did mine on my own."

"Who helped her?"

"She had this aunt, a professional artist. I don't want to talk about that," she said abruptly. "You need to know more about kites, kiddo."

She launched into a lengthy explanation about bridles, spars, and someone named Hargrave, who'd invented the box kite. Then out of her collection of goodies, she showed me a picture of a box kite. "It's used for checking the weather and jazz like that. Sometimes, the military puts a person in it."

I studied the photo. I turned to her and said suspiciously, "You don't want me along because you figure I'm small enough to fit into this doohickey, do you?"

She cracked up. "You've got to be kidding!" She paused. "Though that's an idea." She looked at my

75

horrified face and hooted.

We placed newspaper all over the floor of my room. She grabbed a stick and scissors and said gleefully, "Now the fun begins!"

Daddy didn't agree with that when he came home that evening. He stood at the threshold of the room, rubbing his moustache. "Um, did you finish?"

My room looked finished; in fact, it looked mugged. The newspaper still doubled as a rug, but there were pieces of wood everywhere, plus globs of paste, and half the kite, which was monster-sized, graced the middle of the room.

"Not according to Rachel."

"Well, you're the one who has to sleep here," he said with a chuckle. "I thought we'd go to the animal shelter on Saturday unless you have a game or something."

"No. Oh, wow! I told Mom about it, and she thinks it's a neat idea. She really loved Gilligan, did you know that?"

"I knew," he replied. "I gave her Gilligan when we were first married. To keep her company while I was on the road. It didn't help much," he added sadly. He'd moved into the room a bit. "Yecch!" He lifted his right foot. On the bottom of his crepe sole was a slice of baloney covered with mayo.

"Rachel's after-school snack. I'm sorry. I'm not finished cleaning up."

"You may graduate from high school before you get done cleaning this place."

"I've decided to get a grown cat. Mom said kittens are fun but if you get involved with something or aren't around, they can get into lots of mischief. She said she was doing some sketches for school once and Gilligan wandered into the kitchen and managed to get himself tangled up in the cafe curtains. I wouldn't want to leave a little cat all by himself while we're out."

"My, my, very grown-up sounding. You and your mother had a good weekend, didn't you?"

"Yes."

"Maybe she's doing some growing up, too."

"Daddy!"

"What's wrong, Cory?"

"It's just . . ." I toed the dirty newspaper. "I just wish you and Mom wouldn't make those cracks about each other. Not to me."

He pursed his lips. "Cory, you might be adjusting to the divorce without any problems, but I'm not you." And with that, he strode from the room.

I winced. Daddy gets funny sometimes. When I least expect it, he can get cold and remote, like now. It doesn't last long and doesn't happen often, but when it does, I know to stay out of his way. I closed the door.

Should I call Rachel and tell her about getting the cat? She might want to come along and picking out a pet was something I wanted to do with Daddy alone. That would upset her. She was still put out because I was going over to Beth's. When we were pasting sticks together, she said real casual-like, "So, the old man's getting soft, huh? Letting you go somewhere after school. Somewhere other than baseball. Cool, kiddo, real cool." Rachel's like that. It's fun for her to bring up stuff when you least expect her to.

On Tuesday, when I was going to the game (with Rachel by my side), Beth came over, "Don't forget tomorrow, Cory. And good luck today."

"'Don't forget tomorrow, Cory. And good luck today.' What a wimp! Such a phony-baloney!"

Ignoring her remarks, I said, "Speaking of baloney, we have to clean up the room better next time. I had *some* job yesterday."

The corners of her mouth turned down. "You didn't move stuff around?"

"Yes, Rachel. I couldn't find my bed."

"Kiddo, everything was in its proper place. Who cares about a bed? Sleep on the floor—"

"I couldn't find that, either."

"A minor inconvenience for a few days."

"A few days, Rachel? The contest is over the Memorial Day weekend. That's two-and-a-half weeks away. I need my bed. Trust me, Rachel."

We both laughed. "You're okay, kiddo. A little bit of a mouse, but okay."

Cory Mouse. Sounded like a comic strip. Why not? Sometimes I thought I was a living cartoon. Only I wasn't writing the balloon lines myself.

St. Luke's was a better team and they won by a score of nineteen-to-ten. I managed a couple of steals, a sacrifice bunt, and I threw a lead runner out at third. I also got creamed by a line drive, tripped in the muddy infield, and ran into my own lead runner, Binky, at home. He apologized. "I'm getting a new boa constrictor. That's all I can think about. Sorry, Cory."

"It's okay, Binky," I said, wiping myself off. "The run didn't mean much. I'm getting a cat so I know how distracted you can get."

"Thanks," he said. "I may bring the boa to school one day. Maybe you'll bring your cat, too?"

"Maybe. But not on the same day."

He grinned and so did I.

Rachel didn't show up at the elevator the next morning. I trooped to her door. As soon as I rang the bell, the "poodies" yipped. They went on like that for what seemed like forever. The Fourth Mrs. Vellars finally answered the door. She wore a lavender robe, her hair was in orange rollers, and oil was smudged on her face. Between yawns from her and barks from the dogs, she informed me that Rachel wouldn't be in school today. Before I could speak, she slammed the door in my face. Some lady!

It wasn't unusual for Rachel to take a day off, even when she wasn't sick. "I need time to recharge my batteries. Too much Markham wears on me." Her parents never objected. If I'm not running a temperature or doubled over, I'm forced to go to school. I sort of minded Rachel's not being there. Without her, I had to ride the bus alone, walk through the halls alone, eat by myself, and go home alone. But today, I reminded myself, you're going over to Beth's.

"Where's Rachel?" Beth asked when she passed me in the cafeteria. She held a tray full of yogurts.

"Sick."

"Don't catch it. You're coming over to my apartment today. Or did you forget?"

"Why would I do that?"

"Because you didn't say anything in D.A."

"Oh, I was too worried there."

"About what?"

"About blowing up that air-conditioning unit Mrs Lindsey had us working on. I don't think I'm cut out to be a repairperson. Mrs. Lindsey isn't, either."

Beth smiled. "What do you think you're cut out for?" she asked, sliding into Rachel's usual place.

"Um, I don't—"

"Don't tell me now. Later. Just think about it. Okay?"

What was she acting so mysterious about? Something to do with my visit, I bet. I wanted to change the subject. "Reducing Markham to rubble wasn't the only problem on my mind. It's my turn to contribute a recipe. I was supposed to get one from my mother over the weekend, but we were having such a good time that we both forgot."

"That's easy enough to fix," Beth said brightly. "We'll come up with a recipe at my house. Don't worry, Cory. Here, have a banana yogurt," she smiled again and returned to her table.

She pointed to me and Frannie and Amanda stared. I looked at the yogurt. Had I accidentally been given someone's lunch? I glanced at them a second time. Frannie waved and Amanda gave me a thumb's up sign. I had a hunch they'd turn up at Beth's. Well, they looked friendly enough. Maybe Jenny had over-reacted. Absently, I dug into the container. It wasn't until I swallowed that I remembered I hate banana yogurt.

Chapter 10

"My mother's at the beauty parlor," Beth announced when I entered the apartment. She led me through a bright foyer. "My brother, Alexander, is in his room. He has his Walkman on and unless we're attacked by Tomato People, he won't know we're here." She now entered the butcher block and chrome-accented kitchen.

"This is nice," I said.

"Yeah, I love being in here, especially when Mother is cooking. She's really a gourmet," Beth said with pride. She opened the fridge and took out two sodas, removed tall glasses from the cabinet above the sink, and from another cabinet came up with a bag of pretzels.

I sat on one of the chrome chairs. "You haven't had to bring in a recipe yet."

"I'm the only one. Mrs. Lindsey must be afraid to ask me," Beth giggled.

"Why?" I hoisted my canvas tote on the table.

"Because my mother always comes up with some fancy dish for the teachers' dinners and special occasions."

I nodded. Parents were asked to contribute to dinners, luncheons, and even a big party at a local Holiday Inn. Daddy sent a check.

"Then I guess the recipe you're going to help me with isn't from your mother's files."

"Don't worry, Cory. Amanda and Frannie will come up with something. We'll all work on it together."

That meant the others would be here. Would I be placed under a microscope? It was too late to back out now. I sipped my soda.

Beth was quiet, too. It was a nice silence, but I'm so used to Rachel's noisiness that I had to speak. I rummaged through the bag. "Um, here are some pictures. Pictures of Gilligan." I slid over the Polaroid shots. "They were taken over the years. That's where I used to live. It's tiny, isn't it? My mom still lives there. Actually, it doesn't look so small anymore with just Mom in the apartment." I was babbling because Beth's mouth had formed a large *O* when I showed the photos.

"See, Gilligan loved to sit by the window. With the screen in, though." My voice caught slightly but I kept going. "He also liked to shred Mom's drawings. He used them as a scratching post. In this shot, she's glaring at him. He's just ripped up some drawings. But she never stayed angry with him—"

"Stop!" Beth said, sliding off the chair next to mine and running off.

I blew it. She's in her room, crying her eyes out about Fluffy. Back in my apartment, it seemed like such a good idea to bring over the photos. They'd give us something to talk about. I could show myself out.

Beth flew back into the room, a fistful of pictures in her hand. In the other, was a small, tattered green blanket. "This was Fluffy's. She always kneaded on it."

"Gilligan liked to make doughnuts, too."

"'Make doughnuts?' That's neat!" She beamed and sat next to me again.

We started talking at the same time and our sentences overlapped, and we understood everything the other said. I told her about my life in New York; she'd lived in Port Hudson all her life but had moved to the

Towers three years ago, the same time Markham opened. Before that, she'd attended a terrible private school.

"It was right out of Charles Dickens," she said with a grimace. "I think Fagin ran the place. Oh, he's—"

"A rotten character in *Oliver Twist*. I love that story," I said excitedly. No one else my age ever knew anything about Charles Dickens. He was my favorite author, even if some of his books were hard for me to read.

"I've never read it," she admitted. "But my father is a Dickens' fan and we have the video cassettes of all the movies that were made from Dickens' novels."

"I love *A Christmas Carol*," I said and we both said in unison, "The original movie." And broke up.

I heard the door open. Heels clicked on the wood floor in the foyer, then on the kitchen tiles. I caught my first glimpse of Mrs. Lowery. She was short and a little on the heavy side. My eyes widened. She wore a VMC cotton suit.

Beth jumped up and kissed her mother. "Ugh-pee-yew! You stink of hairspray." She stepped away.

"Unfortunately, the bees in the shopping center parking lot didn't agree with your assessment. They practically buzzed me to death. Hello, I don't know you." She extended her hand. Her grip was firm.

"You don't know me but you're wearing my mother's clothes." I must be hanging out with Rachel too much. What a remark! Quickly, I added, "My mom is Virginia Matthewson. The designer. Your suit. Number 9876. I have a scaled-down version."

Mrs. Lowery's pleasant laugh filled the room. "This is the nearest I've ever been to a designer. Virginia Matthewson is my all-time favorite. She really understands the needs of a short woman."

"She is one."

"What's your name?"

"I'm sorry, Mother. This is Cory."

"Cory, Elizabeth told me how understanding you were about poor Fluffy." When she mentioned the cat, she looked sad.

"Cory was a big help, Mother. Look, she brought over pictures of her cat, Gilligan. He died, too. Wasn't he pretty?"

Mrs. Lowery studied the pictures. I liked her. Maybe she'd sit down and talk with us. My hopes were dashed when the doorbell chimed. Even from inside the apartment, the laughter was unmistakable. Beth answered the door. Amanda and Frannie suddenly filled up the kitchen. They didn't pay any attention to Mrs. Lowery or the photographs.

Amanda said, "Hi, Cory." Frannie smiled.

"You girls can have snacks in Elizabeth's room," Mrs. Lowery said. "But out of my kitchen. I have a meal to prepare."

The other three flew out. I hung back. "Um, I have to put the pictures back in my bag."

"Of course." And Mrs. Lowery helped. When all the shots were inside the tote, she said kindly. "They won't eat you, Cory."

I gave a small smile and ambled down the hall. Beth was in the doorway, ushering me inside. Her room was slightly larger than mine. She had a big four poster and two foam roll outs. For sleepovers, I bet. The walls were pale orchid—what you could see of the walls, that is. They were covered with posters of Smurfs, E.T., Ewoks, and Broadway plays.

"My father works in the theater. Something to do with publicity. That's how I get all of those," Beth explained.

Everyone had plopped onto the floor. I did, too.

"Now, before we get to Cory's recipe for D.A., there's something else we have to do," Beth said.

Uh-oh. I remembered her cryptic remarks in the cafeteria. *"What do you think you're cut out for? . . . Don't tell me now. Later. Just think about it,"* This was definitely later.

"Yes!" Amanda clapped her hands.

"This will be so much fun," Frannie said breathlessly.

"What will be?" I asked.

Beth replied, "Real and fantasy. It's a game we play."

"A board game?" I asked hopefully. They were always fun.

"No," Amanda answered. "You have to tell us what you really want to be when you grow up and also what you would be if you could be anything you wanted. Anything at all!"

I thought for a second. "Well, my fantasy—"

"No!" Frannie squealed. "You can't tell us, Cory. You have to show us."

"Charades?" I said, feeling my stomach lurch. If there was any game on earth I hated, it was charades. Ginny McNeil had had this huge family of a zillion aunts, uncles, cousins, and in-laws, and they'd get together a few times a year and there'd always be charades. They insisted I play. I always got terribly embarrassed and in front of all those people, I could barely recall my own name.

"It's fun, Cory," Beth said. "There aren't any rules.

Just that you have to act out your real wishes and your fantasy ones."

"Acting out is probably as close as I'll ever come to my wish," Amanda said. "But you can't know my dreams yet, Cory. You first."

Slowly, I got to my feet. Cory Matthewson. Yes, that was my name. And there were only three kids here, not seventy-five relatives and friends. "Um, I'll do the fantasy, okay?"

"Sure, sure," Frannie said.

I took a deep breath. That make-believe wouldn't be that hard. If I didn't trip over my sneakers while acting out. I assumed a familiar stance.

"A baseball player!" Amanda shouted.

"What position?" Beth wanted to know.

I put my hand up to my head and used the other hand in traffic—cop style. Amanda said, "Shortstop! Oooh, you're good at this, Cory."

"But you're already a shortstop," Frannie said.

"This is her grown-up fantasy," Amanda reminded her. "You play the piano now but your make-believe is that you're a world famous pianist. Ooops, I shouldn't have said that. Frannie should have acted it out. Sorry."

"That's okay," Beth said. "I think Cory's fantasy is terrific. There aren't any women major leaguers."

"I don't think there ever will be," I said. "Ooops, was it okay for me to talk?"

The three of them laughed. "Sure," Beth said. "But now do your real wish."

I stood there. And stood there.

"When are you going to start?" Amanda asked.

I nodded.

"You already have?" she sounded surprised. Then Amanda nodded, too. "You don't know what you want to be."

"Right."

"No ideas?" Beth asked. I shook my head. "Well, that's okay. Our real and fantasy wishes change from time to time."

"With you, it's everytime we play," Amanda said. "Last time it was a real estate tycoon, before that, a movie producer, before that—"

"But she's always rich and powerful," Frannie put in.

That didn't surprise me. Beth was a definite leader. I sat down. Amanda got up. It was much more fun guessing what someone else was acting out than being up there myself. Amanda's reality was an executive in a cosmetic company but her fantasy surprised me. She yearned to be a housewife.

"No job at all?" I asked. "I don't know what I want

to do but there must be something outside of the home for me."

Amanda said softly, "My mother is a policewoman. I'm always scared when she goes to work that she won't come back. I'd rather be home. But every family seems to need two incomes now."

I was impressed. Amanda seemed deeper than I thought. She was all right.

Since I knew Frannie's dream, all she did was her reality, which was a piano teacher. "But you're so good," I found myself saying. "You could really be a concert pianist, Frannie."

Frannie shrugged. "It takes so much work and I get so nervous sometimes."

I knew how she felt. Frannie was a bit like me.

All in all, I was having a terrific time, talking, acting out, drinking soda, munching on pretzels, and just being with other kids. Then Amanda turned to me and asked breathlessly, "Tell me, Cory, *honestly* now, did you *really* leave a mash note on Delancey's car?"

Uh-oh. Talk about fantasy and reality.

Chapter 11

I whispered, "No, Rachel just made that up." Now Amanda would squeal, "I knew it! I knew it!" And the true story would be out and they'd think me dull and boring.

"I knew it! I knew it!" she squealed. "It sounded like something that awful Rachel Vellars would make up. Absolutely tacky. Not the sort of thing *you* would do, Cory."

Before my face could register total amazement, Frannie nodded, "Yeah, I don't know how you can hang out with Rachel. She's so gross. Not even Mr. Carmichael likes her and he's the nicest teacher I've ever had."

Beth said, "That's because Rachel traced her 'People at Play' assignment from the centerfold of *Playgirl*."

Rachel had gloated over that one for days.

"So, why do you hang out with her, Cory?" Amanda asked.

"Um, we live on the same floor."

"I wouldn't stay with her even then," Amanda said. "I'd rather be friends with Tommy O'Brien."

"Yeah," Frannie echoed.

I stared at the Ewoks poster, thinking how much Rachel would like it, and wishing I could say something in her defense, but the words stuck.

"Look, we all know Rachel's gruesome," Beth said. "That's nothing new. Let's talk about something else."

Did my silence mean that I agreed? Rachel was a bit much. But she was my friend. My only friend. Check that. I looked at the trio. I had more than one friend now. I didn't want to lose them. Defending Rachel just might accomplish that. I remained quiet.

By the time I left, I had the recipe. It was something that came to me all at once. Beth asked if we ever cooked *anything* not in the microwave. I remembered our Sunday brunches. I told the girls about the tradition. They loved the idea. Beth pointed out that Mrs. Lindsey might freak out about the cholesterol level so we decided on poached eggs, sausages that didn't contain preservatives and additives, and the home fries would be cooked in corn oil.

Then they walked me to the Claredon. I felt super. Except for that uncomfortable business about Rachel, they hadn't interrogated me. They'd treated me as an equal.

When we were in front of the building, Frannie said, "I have to give a piano recital Saturday, and I really need you guys for moral support. Promise me you'll be there. Maria said she's coming up."

"Sure thing. You know I wouldn't miss Maria!" Amanda said enthusiastically. "Oh, not that I don't want to hear you play, Frannie," she added apologetically.

"It's just that you hear me all the time and you don't see Maria as much as you used to."

"Right, she was my best friend."

"I'll have to check with my parents," Beth said.

Frannie nodded. "Cory?"

I'd almost forgotten I was there, which sounds impossible, but isn't. When Frannie mentioned the recital, I felt excluded, but with that one little, "Cory?" I was included. Then I remembered—on Saturday, Daddy and I were going to the animal shelter. I toed the gravel. "I'm sorry, Frannie. My dad's taking me somewhere."

"Those are the breaks," Frannie sighed. She didn't

add, "Another time." Would I ever be asked anywhere again?

I thanked them for helping me with the recipe and marched into the building. As soon as I stepped off the elevator, Rachel pounced.

"I spent most of the afternoon playing gin rummy with Mrs. Heffernan. I won two out of three. Bet I had a lot more fun than you and the snobbie-creepos."

I think Rachel only played gin rummy when she was bored to tears. Instantly, I felt guilty for not sticking up for her with the others. I should have said something in her defense. Like maybe mentioning the kite contest and how we were partners. Or even that she's a bubble bath freak.

"You had a lousy time, didn't you, kiddo? I warned you!" she said in a sing-song voice.

"I had a nice time," I said softly.

"Don't lie to me, Cory. I saw your face when you came into the building. You weren't smiling then. Did they kiss you off?"

"How did you see me?"

"Through the opera glasses, naturally. Let's see, you were smiling at first then Frannie said something—I have to learn how to lip read—and then you looked blank. Then you seemed okay. But when you left, I could tell, kiddo, that was the last you'd see of the snobbie-creepos. Just as well."

"Rachel Vellars, how could you? You were spying on me. I'm supposed to be your best friend. That's a terrible, rotten thing to do!"

"Give me a break. You know I always watch people. It's the only way you learn anything."

I didn't reply. Yes, she spied on other people. But on me? That wasn't right. I was beginning to feel less and less guilty about not saying anything in her defense.

"Well, just don't stand there like a lump. Tell me everything. Every little detail!" she rubbed her hands together in anticipation.

By now, I'd reached my door.

"Good, we'll work on the kite."

"Rachel, you can't come in," I said tiredly. I wanted to get away from her. My mind was all jumbled. First feeling sorry for her. Then getting angry with her for spying on me. And now just exhausted.

"Dumb rules. Then don't go inside, kiddo. Tell me out here. C'mon, c'mon!" She practically danced in the hall. "Tell me something they said. *Anything*. Pretty please, with whipped cream on top, the real stuff, not Cool Whip. C'mon, kiddo! Open your mouth!"

I inserted the key in the lock and opened my mouth. The only thing that popped out was, "Everyone agreed that you're gruesome." I walked in and shut the door behind me.

Chapter 12

Rachel was out again on Thursday. I blamed myself. The more I thought about what I'd said to her, the dumber it seemed. But she got me so angry! What right did she have to zing everyone else? She wasn't exactly a perfect person.

Neither was I. But I was trying to improve, to find new friends. Even if they kind of found me.

Mrs. Lindsey approved my menu. She was especially pleased that the cholesterol level had been taken into consideration.

At lunch, I went to my usual table and opened up a tuna sandwich and sipped tart cranberry juice. Beth appeared at my side. "Rachel's out today."

"Yes, it's quiet."

"I noticed that. C'mon, sit with us."

I didn't need a second invitation. I wondered if the other two would mind my being there, but they seemed genuinely pleased to see me. It was super having three people to talk to instead of just one, and Beth and I were on the same wave length about everything.

While we walked to our next class, Frannie asked, "So, are you coming to my recital, Beth? My mother's hired a caterer and she has to know how many people will be there. She's running around like she's organizing a presidential luncheon."

"I can't come, Frannie. My parents have something planned. Even Alexander has been ordered to come along."

The girls shook their heads. Beth's brother hadn't stepped out of his room the entire time I was at her apartment. "You know," I said slowly. "I think Alexander is a figment of everyone's imagination. There is nothing in that extra bedroom except a Walkman attached to a pillow case."

The trio broke up. That made me feel terrific.

"Well, if you don't come, Beth, you'll miss Maria. She'll be disappointed."

"She'll live, Frannie." Did Beth sound less than thrilled with Maria?

"Oh, I can hardly wait to see Maria! Things just haven't been the same without her," Amanda said. "I mean, like she was my best friend in the whole world. Say, Cory, maybe she lives near where you used to— York Avenue?"

"That's the East Side. I lived on the West Side."

"New York is awfully complicated," Beth said thoughtfully. "East, West, Uptown, Downtown. Port Hudson's a lot simpler." Frannie and Amanda nodded.

I slipped into my seat while Mrs. Grinwold barked attendance. Was Port Hudson simpler? Mom and Dad weren't fighting any more. I liked that. I could take the divorce, but all that arguing. Mom screaming that Dad didn't know what was going on because he was never home, and Dad hollering back then getting this disgusted look on his face and storming out the door. It happened all the time in the city. I shivered remembering it. But now—my parents were relaxed. And so was I. Mmmm, Port Hudson was looking better all the time.

Rachel stayed home on Friday, too. That evening, Daddy asked, "Where's the kite flyer? No signs of a tornado having blown through the apartment. No baloney sandwiches stuck to my soles." When I didn't smile at his jokes, he frowned, "What's wrong, Cory? Did you two have a spat?"

"No, she's sick, that's all," I said hurriedly. *Was that all?*

On Saturday morning, I was up at seven. Today I'd get a new cat! I could hardly wait. But I had to since we didn't leave the house 'till ten and our first stop was the library. Usually, I'm excited about going there, but today, it wasn't that exciting. I did pick out a few books on kite flying. Rachel would eventually come around and I wanted to know what we were doing.

Finally, we climbed back into the yellow Honda. It was time to go to the animal shelter. "I have lots of names picked out, Daddy. Smurfy, if it's a boy. Lucy, after Lucy Van Pelt, if it's a girl. Kittenfish, if it's just cute and adorable."

"Since you're getting a grown cat—that is still the plan, isn't it?"

"Yes."

"Well then, a grown cat may already have a name. Not all the animals at the shelter will be strays. Some will have been given names by owners who no longer want their cats."

"That's horrible!" I said, immediately thinking about how unhappy I'd been when Gilligan died and how miserable Beth was about Fluffy. "How could someone just give away a pet?"

"Things happen, Cory. Maybe the owner developed an allergy or became ill in another way and could no longer care for the animal. At the least the owner will have had the decency to bring the cat to the shelter instead of letting it loose on the street. That's cruel," he added.

"Mmmm, I see what you mean."

The shelter was a gray building that took up half a block. There was a reception area inside, plus a place where pet accessories were sold. We were allowed through a gate and into the rear of the building where I went crazy seeing all those puppies, dogs, kittens, and cats. There were thirty animals in all.

"We don't put any healthy animals to sleep here," our guide, a friendly black woman named Mrs. Jackson, told us. "We take care of them all. And try to find good homes for them."

"They look well taken care of," Dad said. "My daughter is looking for an adult cat."

"How wonderful! So many people insist on a young animal when a grown one will make just as nice a companion. We have three lovely cats here," she led us over to spotless cages.

She wasn't kidding. One was cream colored, with long hair. It was a four-year-old male and his name was Oatmeal. The second was an orange tiger and his name was Morris. I could see why. He was a twin for the TV cat. The third was a mess of splotchy colors. Her face was all white, though. She didn't have a name since she was a stray. She was just about a year old. I wanted all three.

Daddy read my mind. "One, pumpkin. Just one."

But which? How could I make up my mind? None

of the cats paid me much attention, which is okay, since that's the way cats are. I studied each. According to Mrs. Jackson, Morris had been at the shelter five days. He was two years old and looked so much like the TV feline that he'd find a home real soon. And the No-Name was just so cute and adorable that someone would jump at the chance to take her home. But Oatmeal was four. Not many people would want a four-year-old pet. And he had all that long hair to brush. He looked like he ate a lot, too. Mrs. Jackson said he'd been here for over a month. That was an awfully long time. No one wanted Oatmeal.

"I'll take him. He's my cat," I said firmly.

Daddy rubbed his moustache. "Are you sure, Cory?"

"Absolutely. He needs me. I can tell." And I needed him.

"Then Oatmeal it will be," Daddy said.

"I'm delighted, Mr. Matthewson," Mrs. Jackson said. "Oatmeal is affectionate. He's part Persian and Angora. His owner loved him very much. She passed on," she added quietly.

I blinked. I'd take real good care of Oatmeal!

There were papers for Daddy to fill out and we had to buy a box and litter and food and a brush and just lots of stuff. Daddy gave me money and told me to go

103

to the store in the building. I leaned over Oatmeal and gently put my fingers in the cage. He sniffed and his whiskers twitched. "I'll be right back. I'll be right back," I repeated. Cats liked to hear people talk. Oatmeal blinked.

I dashed into the front area. A guard cautioned me against running. I blushed and stopped.

"Cory, what are you doing here?"

"Beth, what are you doing here?"

"We came to get a kitten."

"So did I! Well, a cat. A grown one."

"Isn't this nice?" Mrs. Lowery said. She wore another VMC skirt and jacket. "You two should have told each other. We could have pooled together."

"Not with Alexander draped all over the back of the car." Beth sighed. "I swear, his headphones are glued to his ears. My father's outside. He says all the animals make him nervous." Her voice dropped. "Cory, I'm nervous, too. Know what I mean?"

"Yes, but this is a wonderful place. Go find Mrs. Jackson. She's super and knows all about animals."

"Oh, did you find anything?"

"Oatmeal," I said brightly. "That's his name. He's four, has long, long hair, and is just wonderful."

"See, Elizabeth? Cory's found a new pet. Elizabeth wasn't terribly keen on coming here. But now that you're here, I'm sure she's more convinced that this is the right thing."

Beth smiled at her mom and gave her a big hug. "Cory, you'll help me, won't you?"

Being asked to help her pick out her kitten was an honor. But I shook my head. "It's your choice, Beth. You have to find a kitten just for you. I can't do that for you. There are four really cute kits back there. Do you understand?"

"Yeah, I know exactly what you mean. Can you wait for me, though? I want to see Oatmeal, too."

"Great, fine. See you later," I said as Mrs. Lowery and Beth went through the gate. Imagine meeting Beth here and imagine her wanting *me* to help her out. Port Hudson sure was looking better all the time.

Chapter 13

Oatmeal would have the run of the apartment once he got used to the place. Meanwhile, he stayed in my room, litter box, food dish, water bowl, and toys. Mrs. Jackson suggested we feed him canned food since that's what his last owner gave him. Daddy gags at the smell of canned cat food; Mom used to feed Gilligan. So, I had a new job.

Oatmeal was fun to watch. Not that he did much. Ate, used the box (which I promptly cleaned out), and slept. I'd hoped he'd sleep with me but as soon as it got dark, he disappeared under the bed. It would take time. He must be frightened in new surroundings. I'd be patient with him. I hoped he'd be patient with me, too.

He was still under the bed when I took my Sunday morning bubble bath. I *love* bubble baths. Mom gives me new fragrances and Rachel is forever swapping with me. Today I was using the one that smelled like a Christmas tree. That was Rachel's favorite, too. I kicked my feet, splashing bubbles on the tiles. I missed Rachel. I wanted to share with her all the stuff that went on with Beth, Frannie, and Amanda. But she wouldn't want that. Why was she so difficult? I kicked again. She was sure taking time recharging her batteries. Or was there something more to it? Like she was really hurt by me? I didn't want to think about that. I concentrated on the evergreen aroma. It always makes me feel like something super is about to happen.

When I came out of the tub, I walked into my room. Oatmeal was on the bed, making doughnuts on the coverlet. His rumbly purr filled the room. I tiptoed over and gently sat on the bed. He glanced at me through sleepy green eyes. I touched him softly. He rubbed his head in my hands. Something wonderful had happened.

Later, I had to take the garbage out to the incinerator. Daddy couldn't stand having the empty cans in the kitchen. Mr. and Mrs. Vellars strode out of the elevator. They both carried golf clubs.

"I'll never play with that Finch again. He cheats, you know. He didn't score any birdie on the fifth hole," Mr. Vellars grumbled. He looks like a better-put-together Rachel, but still gangly and awkward.

"Cory, haven't seen you around much lately."

"What is that foul odor?" Mrs. Vellars demanded, wrinkling her long nose.

"Cat food. We have a new cat."

"My poodies don't like cats," she said.

"Why haven't you been around? Rachel's ill, you know. Has some sort of a bug. I had to call the doctor on Thursday. They still make house calls. Charge outrageously for them, too. Don't know if she'll be in school tomorrow."

"I hope she is!" Mrs. Vellars moaned. She seemed to be collapsing under the weight of the clubs. Her husband shot her a dirty look. "Adam, I cannot take it! She's boisterous even when ill. I cannot be expected to wait on her hand and foot!"

"She's my daughter and I pay Gwendolyn a king's ransom to wait on both of you hand and foot," he said evenly. Then he remembered I was still there. "Good day, Cory," he said abruptly. Mrs. Vellars didn't speak; she just followed her husband.

I hung back, waiting for them to get inside their apartment before going to the incinerator. Why'd I get the impression that Rachel might lose another stepmother? It wouldn't be a great loss. I wouldn't like someone like The Fourth Mrs. Vellars around.

After depositing the garbage, I realized something.

Rachel hadn't been avoiding me. She'd really been sick. I felt funny about that. After the rotten thing I'd said to her. I'd go see her later.

When I stepped inside our apartment, the telephone rang. It was Beth. "Cory, you should see Sleeky! She's so funny! She tried to climb the drapes. And she actually got Alexander to stop listening to his Walkman for five minutes. That's because she played tug-o-war with the wires."

I giggled. I'd met Sleeky yesterday. She was an eight-week-old kitten, all black with gold eyes. She got her name when Beth said, "Isn't she slinky?" at the same time I uttered, "Wow, is she sleek!" I was proud of having helped name her.

"She's into everything. How about Oatmeal?"

"Lumpy. He just sits around. He's an older cat. He won't get into much mischief." And with that brilliant statement, something in my room crashed. "I have to go. Oatmeal just stopped being lumpy."

Beth laughed. She understood. It was great not needing to explain my every sentence.

I hung up and dashed into my room. Oatmeal had knocked off all the library books from my desk. He was now perched there, cleaning himself. The books had fallen near the half-finished box kite, but the kite was okay. Thank goodness! Rachel would have my head. "All right, Oatmeal. The desk is yours." I scratched him behind the ears and on the chin. He loved that.

After brunch, I went to visit Rachel. Daddy didn't question me. He was too occupied with a new program for the computer. The "poodies" yelped when I rang the bell. Mrs. Vellars, in a magenta robe, answered the door. The dogs nipped at her floppy slippers.

"Didn't Adam and I see you earlier?"

"Yes. Mr. Vellars told me Rachel was sick. I came to see her. She's not expecting me. I hope she's not contagious," I added quickly.

"I hope she's not! I've been at her beck and call and in and out of *that* room." She shuddered.

I was inside the duplex. The dogs sniffed me. "It's a cat. His name is Oatmeal. He's bigger than both of you and has long, long claws." They yipped once, wagged their funny tails, and scooted after Mrs. Vellars. The poodles weren't that bad. But her? I'd rather have Lizzie Borden for a stepmother.

Rachel was propped up in bed, watching a video cassette of *The Price Is Right*. A chubby bald man in a banana-colored suit won an itty-bitty moped and flew up and down the stage screaming, "I won! I won!"

Exactly how Rachel would act if we won the kite contest. Not me.

As soon as she saw me, she flicked off the cassette via remote control, and boomed, "C'mon in, kiddo! A friendly face! The old man checked in awhile ago, gave me twenty bucks, told me to spend it wisely, and split." She sighed, poked at the covers, then said, "Will you come closer already? I'm not contagious."

"Then what's that doing here?" I pointed to the vaporizer on her cluttered night table. I inched my way into the room and sat on the beanbag chair.

"Oh, that. I needed it at first. I was all congested and yucky. Doctor gave me a shot. That helped more than that thing." She thumbed to the machine. "*That* was The Fourth Mrs. Vellars' idea. I don't think she cared about my cold. She probably figured the vaporizer would get rid of the dust in the room."

"She figured wrong," I said, writing my name on the floor dust.

Rachel laughed. "So, where've you been, kiddo?"

Had she forgotten what I said to her last time—about everyone agreeing that she was gruesome? No. She'd decided to let it go. For now. Rachel had a way of bringing up something when you least expected it.

"I've been busy. We got a new cat."

She practically flew out of bed. "C'mon, c'mon! I want to see it!"

"No."

"What do you mean?"

"Rachel, maybe you're not contagious to me, but I don't know if Oatmeal could catch what you have."

She settled back into bed. "Mmmm, yeah. Animals can get diseases from people. I read that in the *Nosybody*. Oatmeal. That's a pretty good name."

I grinned. Suddenly, she was asking a million questions about him, school, and even baseball. But nothing specific about Beth, Frannie, and Amanda.

"And don't forget about the contest, kiddo. We have to finish that kite. We'll work on it tomorrow afternoon. You can lug the stuff over here. That way, we don't get germs on Oatmeal, and we drive The Fourth right up the walls."

"Tuesday, not tomorrow."

"Why?" she bellowed. "You got *other* plans?"

"There's a game. We should beat this team. We have to beat someone. Eventually."

"You hope," Rachel said. "Tuesday then. I'll stay home again tomorrow. Maybe. Anyhow, we have to get the kite finished by Memorial Day."

Mom had custody of me on that weekend but she'd begged off. I think she has a boyfriend and has plans with him. But she hasn't actually told me about him yet. When we were at the Lime Banana, Giorgio was there with his family, and he asked how Teddy was. Mom blushed and I guessed Teddy was someone special. That was fine with me, but Mom didn't volunteer any information. Adults can be awfully secretive when they want to.

"We still have to make the reel and put on decorations."

"Decorations?"

"Yeah, and do I ever have a super idea, kiddo. You know how I told you box kites are used for weather jazz?" I nodded. "I figure weather is close enough to astrology, so we're going to have zodiac signs on the box."

Only Rachel would associate weather "jazz" with signs of the zodiac. "Super."

"Yeah, we're going to be working all the time this coming week. Don't you forget that."

I wouldn't, but I might want to.

Chapter 14

Rachel stayed out on Monday. I had lunch with Beth, Frannie, and Amanda.

"I have to stay late," Amanda said. "Mrs. Albert wants to go over my mistakes on the last history test. That's the whole test," she added with a small smile. "I'm terrible in history."

"Why don't you ask Cory for help?" Beth suggested.

"Yeah, you're a whiz in it," Amanda said brightly. "What's your secret? A photographic memory for all those *boring* dates?"

"I don't try to remember the dates," I said. "They just surround the stories, like commercials."

"Huh?" They all said in unison.

I sipped at my orange soda before replying. "My mom, she gave me this idea—her mother gave it to her—when I had trouble with history once." The three girls looked at me expectantly. I hoped they didn't think it was a dumb story. "She told me to ignore the dates and concentrate on the *story* of history. To follow it like the plot of a TV program. She got me all caught up in people's lives instead of worrying about what date I had to remember."

"You mean like the Russian tsars are an hour show or something?" Amanda asked.

"Yes. I'd read about them, close my eyes, and picture the show, from the opening credits to the closing theme music. It's fun. And it makes history come alive."

Beth was thoughtful. Frannie just smiled. Amanda wanted to know, "But what about the dates being commercials?"

"Oh, Mom said there was no getting away from commercials. After awhile, you got used to them and even memorized most of them—"

"The way you can eventually memorize dates," Amanda said, clapping her hands. "Great, Cory! That makes so much sense. I'm going to try it. Thanks."

"Yeah, it is a neat idea," Beth said.

"Right," Frannie said.

I blushed. Beth said, "I'm staying after school, too. I'm going to root for Cory. She says the Eagles will finally win a game."

"Well, if everyone else will be here, so will I," Frannie said. "I'll root for Cory, too. Just tell me when to cheer, Bethie. I don't know anything about baseball. Except for half time."

Beth and I glanced at each other and she winked. Friends at the game. That was so terrific!

But for the first time, I was edgy. What if I ripped my pants sliding into second or bunted for a third strike? Please, let everything be okay.

And it was better than that. I stole three bases, beat out a bunt, and even got a double out of a Texas league blooper. We won eighteen-to-fourteen. Our first!

Mrs. Winchell congratulated all of us. "Fine game. Great sacrifice fly in the fourth, Tommy. Binky, I couldn't believe that catch you made in the second. You saved two runs."

"I couldn't believe it, either," he said. "I was trying to duck away from the ball and it plopped into my glove."

Laughter. Mrs. Winchell turned to me. "Cory, what can I say? You were magnificent. You always are."

"Yeah, she really understands the finer points of the game," Binky said. From someone who was an expert on such things, that was high praise.

To my surprise, everyone cheered and applauded. Wow! What a great day this was turning out to be.

"I'll drive you kids home in ten minutes," Mrs. Winchell said.

Beth met me outside the field. "We have to celebrate."

"I think I'll celebrate with a shower." My uniform was caked with mud.

"Fine, we have a shower at my apartment, too, you know. Frannie already said she'd be over. She went to get Amanda."

Sounded super. Only Daddy hadn't okayed it. I was to go straight home from the game. I was going to tell Beth that when Amanda and Frannie arrived. Telling all of them that my father didn't allow me to go somewhere after school unless he knew about it beforehand sounded so babyish. What could I say? Then it came to me. "I have to get home to Oatmeal. He hasn't been fed today." That sounded cruel. I added, "Well he had half a can, but he eats more than that."

"We'll just have to celebrate another day," Beth said.

"Thursday at my house. Guess who's coming up?" Amanda asked. A huge smile crossed her face.

"Maria!" Frannie said excitedly.

"Yeah, she has a half day because of some teachers' conference. Her mother's coming up to see her sister.

117

Maria's aunt lives on my block," Amanda added, obviously for my benefit. And Maria's aunt was probably the artist Rachel had complained about.

"And Cory just has to meet Maria. They're vice-versas," Amanda said.

"Huh?" Frannie asked.

"Amanda means I came up to Port Hudson from Manhattan in October about the same time Maria moved from here to the city. Vice-versas."

Amanda's eyes twinkled. I think she was pleased I understood what she meant. "So, you can't miss Thursday, Cory. Don't forget to give your cat plenty of food in the morning."

I managed a weak smile as I said good-bye and headed for Mrs. Winchell's car. Daddy would okay it. But what about Rachel? I mean, we were supposed to be working on the kite every afternoon.

Rachel returned to school on Tuesday. I sat with her on the bus and had lunch with her. I missed being with the others, particularly Beth. Then that afternoon, Rachel and I carted all the kite stuff to her apartment. She thought Oatmeal was neat but scared him by diving after him under the bed.

"We're a cinch to win that contest, kiddo," she said after we'd been working for an hour. Her room was its usual mess and worse because of the newspapers on

118

the floor, the paste had overturned, and there were a zillion crayons everywhere. We'd been drawing some of the zodiac signs. My Sagittarius looked like a puny cupid instead of a strong archer. I was tired of pasting and coloring; I sat on the misshapen beanbag and watched Rachel work.

"Thursday we'll have our dry run."

"I can't on Thursday."

"Aw, don't tell me you have another game, kiddo? Look, the Eagles won once. That's all they ever manage. Tell Winchell you have a sore muscle or something. Baseball players are always coming down with something stupid. Why should you be any different?"

"Because I don't have a sore muscle," I said evenly, though I wanted to scream.

"Don't get bent out of shape, kiddo. But this dry run business is important. And you're the one who'll operate the reel. We'll make that tomorrow. I kind of get tangled up in my own feet, but you have good balance, kiddo—"

"Rachel, on Thursday, I'm going over to Amanda's."

She glared. "*Amanda's?* You've got to be kidding!"

The beanbag chair was decidedly uncomfortable. I think the scissors had stabbed it and some of the beans were dribbling out. "She invited me," I whispered.

"Kiddo, you're a glutton for punishment. I thought

you'd have had your fill of the snobbie-creepos by now. They don't *really* like you."

I ignored the last part and said, "They're not snobbie-creepos."

"Amanda-face is the biggest phony going. Except for Maria."

"She's going to be at Amanda's."

Rachel pretended to slit her throat with an aquamarine crayon. "Maria and Amanda, huh? The old third degree. They'll probably use a rubber hose and stick solid steel toothpicks under your nails."

I jumped up. Beans ran all over the newspaper-covered floor. "They will not."

Rachel blinked. "Kiddo, you don't really like them, do you?"

I hesitated. I knew I liked Beth; she was the kind of friend I'd always wanted. Frannie? Maybe. She never said that much. Amanda? Yes. The more I got to know her, the less standoffish she was. Maria was a total mystery. Yes, she frightened me, too, but with Beth there, everything would be okay.

"Cat got your tongue?" Rachel demanded. "Forget about those jerks, kiddo. We got the contest. That comes first. *You promised.*"

I hated arguments. They made my stomach flip-flop

and my mouth and thoughts run on a collision course. "I'll help you tomorrow and Friday," I said quietly.

Rachel scrambled to her feet. Not only was her neck covered with aquamarine crayon but also her hands were gummy from the paste and she had splinters on the hem of her workshirt. "Don't you *dare* fink out on me now, kiddo. Thursday."

"I can't. Tomorrow and Friday. I promise."

"What the heck good is your promise?" Her voice boomed through the duplex. The dogs yapped. "Listen, kiddo," she took a giant step toward me and shook a bitten fingernail in my face. "You help me Thursday *or else.*"

I was terrified. Rachel was threatening me. How could she? I was her best friend. Her only friend. It was then that the collision course between my mouth and thoughts got into full gear and banged together. "No, you listen, Rachel—I have something else planned for Thursday. Something important to me. If you don't like it . . . well . . . tough!" I think I gnashed my teeth together. Whatever I did, they hurt.

"You little mouse-creepo!" she shouted. The barking got louder. Human footsteps followed. "You're no better than the rest of 'em! You all deserve each other. Don't say I didn't warn you, mouse-creepo."

I always hated when she called me kiddo, but mouse-creepo was much worse. Tears began to stream down my cheeks.

"Can't take it, huh, stupid crybaby? They said I was gruesome. You all agreed on that, huh?"

There it was. She finally decided to bring it up. Her timing was fantastic.

"Is everything all right in there, children?" came the timid voice of The Fourth Mrs. Vellars.

Rachel ignored her. "You said you all agreed I was awful. That meant you, too, huh?"

I hadn't agreed with them. But I hadn't protested, either. And right now, I was glad I hadn't. She was horrid, worse than I ever imagined. "Forget it, Rachel! I won't be here Thursday or Wednesday or any—"

"Good! I don't want you working on my kite anymore. I don't want you around at all, stupid mouse-creepo!" And she stormed to the door and yanked it open. Her stepmother's eyes grew wide. "Out of my way!" Rachel bellowed.

The woman jumped backwards. I think I might have felt sorry for Mrs. Vellars if I wasn't feeling so sorry for myself.

I hurried past her, hoping Rachel wasn't lurking in the hall ready to pounce. But Rachel had disappeared.

I ran out of the apartment and into my own. Oatmeal, who now had full run of the place, greeted me. With a soft meow, he curled himself around my feet.

"Who needs Rachel Vellars? I have new friends! Better friends. Right?" I couldn't stop shaking.

Chapter 15

Neither Rachel nor Beth was at the bus stop in the morning. But when Clem pulled up, thundering footsteps filled my ears. Rachel pushed past me. I slowly boarded the bus.

"This whole seat is taken, mouse-creepo," she announced loudly. "Go find somewhere else to sit." And for good measure, she threw her legs over my seat. Her left sock had a hole near the top.

I wondered where I could sit. Beth wasn't around. There was an empty seat near Tommy and Binky but when I got near them, they were talking about a horror movie and yellow gut slime. I'd had an egg for breakfast.

"Cory! Come here! The bus is moving!"

"And all of you kids are supposed to be seated," Clem growled.

Amanda beckoned me. I hurried over. "You've finally seen the light, huh, Cory?"

"The light?"

"About Rabbit-Face Raunchy Rachel."

"Oh, mmmm." And she's seen the light about me, too. But I sure didn't say that.

"I'm glad. She's not the right sort for *us*."

Us. I glanced at Amanda. She was including me.

"She's gruesome," Frannie whispered.

"A perfect description," Amanda said. "Even Clem doesn't like her. He's reported her over and over again. Doesn't do any good. I mean, you'd think even Rabbity Rachel would listen to what Mr. Delancey has to say. But she ignores him, too." Amanda sighed. So did Frannie.

I didn't want to discuss Rachel. "Where's Beth?"

"She has the bug," Amanda answered. "She can't get out of bed."

I was about to say she probably had what Rachel had had but Frannie cut me off. "Bethie can't play with her cat, either. Her mother put it in Alexander's room."

"I wonder if Sleeky will learn how to operate the 'mute' switch on the Walkman?" I said.

We were on safe territory and the remainder of the short ride was comfortable.

The rest of the day was neat with me getting back two test papers with nineties on them. We also cooked my menu in D.A. I was kind of scared that Mrs.

Lindsey would give me another partner, like Rachel, since Beth was absent. She did assign me another partner; luckily, it was Jenny. She didn't say much but we worked nicely together. Too bad she wasn't older. That's probably why the girls had treated her the way they had. Eleven-year-olds were pretty superior to me when I was nine-and-a-half, too. The girls weren't snobbie-creepos. They were age snobs. I could live with that.

I avoided Rachel on the bus and even hung around outside the building until she was inside. When I got in the elevator, it went down to the basement. Was Rachel lurking down there, ready to get me? I gulped when the door opened. Then I sighed. It was only Mrs. Heffernan. She's totally square-shaped and always wears a loose-fitting, brightly colored dress. I don't know how she manages to keep it so spotless when she stays in the basement and storage area all day. Daddy said there was a beautiful office down here, but I never saw it. Mrs. Heffernan always sat at a rickety card table a few feet from the elevator. She liked to keep an eye on what was going on.

"The kite stuff is here if that's what you're looking for."

"I didn't come down here. I mean, the elevator did. Not me."

She blinked. "Ah, someone's fooling with the buttons again." And I could imagine who. The someone who'd used the elevator before I did. "Like I said, the kite stuff is in the storage area. Said she didn't want to see it in her room any longer." Mrs. Heffernan laughed. "Bet that pleased her ditzy stepmother."

Someone on another floor banged on their elevator door. "Let it go," Mrs. Heffernan ordered, fairly yanking me out of the car.

"But I don't want the kite stuff."

She gazed at me through sleepy eyes. "You don't? But the Vellars kid, she told me the two of you were working together this year. Pretty keyed up about winning, too. She almost won last year but that la-di-da kid beat her out. Just between you and me, I don't believe for one moment that la-di-da made that fancy kite herself."

Maria. And I'd meet her tomorrow. "Um, Rachel and I aren't partners anymore, Mrs. Heffernan." I quickly punched for the elevator. "I don't know what Rachel's going to do about the contest."

"Well, I'll be!" Mrs. Heffernan shook her frizzy graying head. "That Vellars kid didn't say anything about that. She usually never shuts up. I'll tell you, I think it's a crying shame."

"That she never shuts up?"

"No, that you two ain't working together anymore. You'd be a tough team to beat. And, that Vellars kid needs someone besides a tubby, grumpy, old woman to lean on. I thought you were the ticket, Matthewson." She shook her head again. "And I'm usually a good judge of character." Then she waddled back to her card table.

I jumped into the car when it arrived. It wasn't my fault. It really wasn't. Rachel was so pigheaded! Yet, I couldn't help but wonder about what the building manager had said. "You'd be a tough team to beat." Would we? Did we have a chance in the contest? I sighed. I'd never know.

On Thursday, my stomach leapfrogged. I'd be riding the bus to Amanda and Frannie's stop, which was the last one. We'd go together to Amanda's house. Beth was still out. I'd called last night, but she had a bad sore throat and couldn't come to the phone. I told Mrs. Lowery a funny story about Oatmeal and she promised to tell Beth.

Amanda lived on Mason Drive, which was adjacent to the Hudson. The air was heavier here, with river odors, but the beautiful weeping willows and stately old houses made me forget the heavy smells. Amanda's house had a huge porch with several chairs and a real hammock. Inside, there was the quiet hum of air conditioning. The furniture was modern and there were splotches of soft pinks and lavenders. Amanda and Frannie led me downstairs to the family room.

Mrs. Fitzgibbons was there, playing Pac-Man. She wore jeans and a T-shirt. She didn't look like a policewoman. Her cheery, lined face grew puzzled when she saw me. Amanda said, "Mother, this is Cory Matthewson. She's new."

Mrs. Fitzgibbons said, "How are you doing?" grinned and returned to her video game. She was really scoring high.

We walked to the opposite end of the enormous room. I wondered two things—one, where was Maria? And two, why had Amanda introduced me as new? I wasn't, though I was new to Mrs. Fitzgibbons.

The doorbell rang. "She's here! She's here!" Amanda squealed.

"I'll get it. My game is over," Mrs. Fitzgibbons said and disappeared upstairs.

"She must have been at her aunt's and spotted us getting off the bus," Amanda said.

Then why didn't she meet us outside? Was she sizing me up? Was she the kind who liked to make a grand entrance? I was expecting a *Seventeen* cover girl at this point, and I wasn't far wrong.

Maria floated down the steps. She wore hot pink,

designer overalls, a red pinstripe shirt, and her thick auburn hair was all feathery and fell nearly to her waist. And she had real curves. This was a sixth grader? She looked more sophisticated than Amanda's sister, Louisa. My palms grew wet and with good reason. The first words out of Maria's mouth were, "So, you're Cory. I was warned you'd be here."

Chapter 16

Maria draped herself over the lumpy couch that took up most of the far wall of the family room. Amanda sat next to her. Frannie was next to Amanda. I could sit on the other side of Maria, but I wasn't sure she wanted me to. Instead, I plopped down on the floor. I removed my Markham blazer.

"Whatever possessed you to move to this sleepy berg from Manhattan, Cory?" were the first words out of Maria's mouth.

"My parents got divorced," I said quietly.

"Yeah, Cory lives with her father in the Claredon. Her mother still lives in the city. Isn't that wild?" Amanda said.

"Yeah, isn't that something?" Frannie said.

"Your father has custody of you? How absolutely *now*. You must tell me, how do you like it?" Maria's voice dropped to a whisper, "And did he get custody of you because your mother is some sort of child beater?"

I reddened. "My dad . . . my mom . . . I mean, everyone figured it would best all around if I lived with Dad."

"You poor, poor child," Maria said. *Child?* I bet I'd be twelve before she would. And the closer I looked, the more positive I was that the bra was mostly padding.

"Your mother doesn't want you. That is so very, *very* pathetic, isn't it?"

Amanda replied, "Very, very," and Frannie said, "Pathetic."

"You know what this reminds me of?" Maria asked then answered herself, "Rachel Vellars. Her mother didn't want her, either. I'm talking about her real mother. The others aren't too crazy about her, either. Can you blame them? I'd desert a freak like Rachel in a minute. That's probably why her father can't keep a wife. With a gruesome kid like that. What do you think of Rachel Vellars, Cory?"

"Um, Rachel and I live on the same floor. We got to know each other." Why couldn't I say, "That's how we became friends"? Because it was difficult getting my mouth to move.

"C'mon, Cory," Amanda urged. "There's more to it. You used to hang out with Rachel."

"That's a true fact," Frannie said with a nod. I stared at her. You can't have a false fact. Frannie wasn't stupid. Probably too overwhelmed by Maria to know what she's saying. I could understand that.

"You poor, poor thing," Maria said. Great, I'd gone from a child to a thing. If only Beth were here. She'd help me out. I had the impression she disliked Maria. Seeing Maria in action, I couldn't blame her. Imagine the number she pulled on poor Jenny. Terrific. She had me saying "poor" now, too. It was contagious.

"I mean, how pitiful it is for you to have a mother who can't abide the sight of you and then having to be friends with a creature like Rachel. You have really had it rough, Cory. You definitely need some sort of protection, doesn't she, Amanda?"

"Definitely, Maria." Frannie nodded again.

"I think you girls can manage it. Of course, *I'll* help you whenever I can. I come up here a lot because of my aunt—she's a well-known artist, you know." Yes, well known at designing kites. "The name Cory Matthewson doesn't sound like it belongs to a wallflower. Don't fret! We'll get you out of your shy and timid being."

"Don't worry, Maria," Amanda said. "We'll do a complete makeover of Cory. You won't recognize her the next time you visit."

A makeover? I'm eleven!

"Very, *very* good, Amanda. And don't you *dare* let her near that gross Rachel again. Rachel is a total freak. Loud and ridiculous. You *must* stay away from her, Cory."

Rachel was loud. Ridiculous? Sometimes. And no worse than the silly way Maria was acting right now.

While the conversation thankfully drifted away from me, I wondered how Rachel would handle this situation?

"Make me over into what, Monkey-Faced Maria? A phoney-baloney, snobbie-creepo like you? Fat chance? I'd rather be me."

Oh, she'd tell Maria off. The sparks would fly! I was sorry Rachel wasn't around. Not just to put down Maria. For me. Amanda and Frannie were nice—when they weren't falling all over themselves to please Maria. And as much as I liked Beth, and I did like her best of all, I missed Rachel's wildness and outrageous comments.

"What do you mean *she* knows about *that?*" Maria's suddenly shrill voice sliced through my thoughts.

I glanced at Amanda, who looked like she wanted to

crawl into the video game. Frannie was holding her breath. Maria glowered. "You know about it!"

"About what?"

"The real-fantasy. Who told you?"

"Beth . . . Amanda and Frannie. They all told me. I think it's neat."

Amanda let out a long sigh, echoed by Frannie. Amanda's green eyes blinked rapidly as she said, "Cory was over at Beth's apartment. She told her about it right away."

"Right away," Frannie said, smiling quickly and showing her dimpled dimples.

"Beth. Well, okay," Maria said. I had a feeling she wasn't too crazy about Beth. Two leaders. Bet they really clashed!

I wiggled my ankles and stood up. "It's getting late. I have to catch the bus."

"*Already?*" Maria asked. "That's too bad." But her eyes and voice didn't look or sound sorry.

"It was nice meeting you, Maria."

"Mmmm."

Amanda walked me upstairs. When we were on the porch, she grabbed my wrist. "It was kind of rough there at the end, but it's okay, Cory. Maria likes you. I'm so glad. Her approval is important."

"Why?"

"Huh?" Then she giggled. "Oh, Cory, you can be so funny sometimes. Maria is worldly. She knows *things*."

How to be mean to people. I couldn't say that to Amanda, though. She was too in awe of Maria. That was rotten. Amanda could be okay when not over-powered by snobbie-creepo Maria. Frannie, too, for that matter. She'd really been a mouse. What about me? I hadn't been much better. Maria was intimidat-ing.

I walked the two blocks to the bus stop alone. I didn't have to face Maria on a daily basis. But I wanted to be friends with Amanda and Frannie, even if they'd acted jerky today.

The bus came right away. There weren't any seats, since it was rush hour. I held onto a pole. I had to poke my way off the jammed bus. It stopped at the corner of the condo community. I glanced up at the Claredon. There was movement in Rachel's bedroom window. She had her opera glasses. Watching me. Oooh, she'd love to hear about what happened this afternoon. And I'd love to tell her. A smile that was growing on my face quickly stopped. I couldn't share my feelings with Rachel. An ache throbbed all over me. Rachel wasn't my friend anymore. I hated that. But what could I do about it?

Chapter 17

Mom called Friday evening and said, "I won't be going away until late Sunday afternoon. Would you like to spend some time with me tomorrow, Cory?"

"Sure, but I have a game." The game was my only planned activity for the Memorial Day weekend. No kite contest, I thought unhappily.

"You know I like baseball."

She sounded anxious. I wondered if Teddy had broken a date or something and that's why she decided to spend the day with me?

Daddy didn't mind that she'd suddenly changed her plans. "I think it's important that she spends time with you, even if she does so in a helter-skelter fashion."

The phone rang again. It was Mrs. Lowery. "Elizabeth still can't talk, but she's coming along, and should be all right by Sunday. We're having an open house then, Cory. We always do on three-day weekends. Shall we expect you and your father?"

Daddy said it sounded like fun. I told her we'd be there. I had something else to do over the weekend. What would Rachel do? Hang out with Mrs. Heffernan? I wasn't sure if the building manager worked over the holiday. I was sure that Mr. Vellars and his wife would take off. They always did—like over the four-day Thanksgiving weekend, they went to Palm Beach, leaving Rachel with Gwendolyn and a frozen turkey. I spent Thursday and Friday in the city, but when I came home, Daddy had a special dinner. I convinced him to let Rachel come by. He wasn't thrilled, especially when she used the drumstick to duel with him, but he let her hang around. She said it was the best Thanksgiving she had ever had.

I wished I had the nerve to phone Mrs. Lowery and ask if Rachel could come, too. She'd probably say yes; she was that nice. Beth wouldn't be overjoyed, though. As much as I liked Beth and knew that we were on the same wave length, I knew she'd never really understand my friendship with Rachel.

What friendship? Rachel didn't want to have anything to do with me. So why was I worrying about her? Because. Just because.

A muggy haze formed over the diamond on Satur-

138

day morning. We lost nineteen-to-four. I walked twice and stole second.

When I came off the field, Mom said, "Cory, it's not important to win, it's how you play the game." I groaned; she sighed. "Corny advice, huh?"

"A little."

"But I am sincerely sorry you lost."

"With this team, that's nothing new. We're kind of like Charlie Brown's All-Stars." Mom gave me a blank stare. Rachel might think comics are for grown-ups, but Mom is one adult who never reads them. "I did my best, though."

"You certainly did. Now, where would you like to have lunch?" Mom led me over to the car. It was a small compact. The rental agency must've loaned it out to demolition derbies. The dents had dents.

"Burger King, I guess."

"You're kidding, Cory."

Mom hates fast food. I pointed to my sweaty, mud-stained uniform. "No other place would let me in dressed like this."

"Then we'll go back to the apartment so you can wash and change."

We climbed into the car. Casually, she said, "I didn't notice Rachel around. No megaphone."

"I haven't seen Rachel much lately except in school," I said, gazing out the window.

"No great loss," Mom said.

"What do you mean by that?" I demanded.

Mom slapped the steering wheel. The car nearly plowed into a mailbox. Mom veered the other way. "Don't get upset with me, Cory, especially not when I'm driving this monstrosity. I simply meant that you have new friends now and won't need to rely on Rachel. Why don't you tell me more about Amanda and Frannie. I already know Beth. She sounds wonderful."

"She is."

"And the other two?"

The air conditioning rattled along with everything else in the car. I tugged at my dirty jersey. "They're okay. I mean, they're Amanda and Frannie."

"I don't get that at all," Mom said as we paused for a light.

"They're both okay," I said tiredly.

"You don't like them?"

"I do. When Maria isn't around."

"Maria? Who's Maria?"

"Someone who used to live in Port Hudson, but who doesn't anymore. She comes up once in while and causes a lot of grief."

"Like Rachel," Mom said.

"Maria's not anything like Rachel!" I said, my voice raising. "She's a snobbie-creepo and says dumb things. 'The name Cory Matthewson doesn't sound like it belongs to a wallflower.' Can you believe that? That doesn't even make any sense. But that's the kind of weird thing Maria says."

"That's not any more peculiar than the things Rachel says."

"Mom, you can't compare Rachel and Maria."

"All right, granted Rachel's had a rough time of it with her mother and father divorced and Mr. Vellars going through wives like they were after-dinner mints, *but*," Mom said strongly as we headed for the underground garage, "that really isn't any excuse for her continued behavior. Look at you, Cory—Daddy and I are divorced, you live with him, but you're not outrageous—"

"Mom, you can't compare me with Rachel, either!"

"Cory, I've had a great deal of experience. I know people."

My stomach felt like it was riding the Dragoncoaster at Playland. "Mom, you may know *people*, but you sure don't know kids. Especially not this kid."

She gasped. We were in the visitor's parking area. As soon as the car wheezed to a stop, I jumped out and

141

dashed for the elevator. I punched the button and it arrived in seconds. I heard Mom's heels clattering on the concrete floor, but ignored them. Inside the car, I pressed five.

Only the elevator stopped one flight up, in the regular basement. The doors opened. One of the tenants stepped in. I got a quick peek at the card table. Mrs. Heffernan was there. So was Rachel. The tenant got out on two and I rode the rest of the way alone. Three floors, just enough time to think.

Daddy didn't notice me; he was engrossed in a computer program. But I had to let him know I was there because Mom would be up in another two minutes. "Daddy."

He nearly jumped through to the sixth floor. "What are you doing here?" he snapped. He hates being interrupted when working on the machine.

I looked away from his angry glare. "Mom and I sort of had a fight."

"I knew it," he muttered. "There goes my peaceful morning. Leave it to Virginia."

"It wasn't entirely Mom's fault. We both said a lot of junk. Then I ran out of the car." My bottom lip trembled.

Daddy's face softened and he rubbed his moustache. "Okay, okay," he sighed.

142

The bell rang and it was Mom. She hurried in. She and Daddy exchanged glances. I prayed they wouldn't get into a shouting match. Or that Daddy wouldn't storm out of the apartment. I had too much to do over the next couple of days and couldn't spare time for one of their fights. But Mom surprised me.

"Jim, it just happened. It was my fault. And Cory's as well. We're simply not connecting today. We had been recently."

"So I heard." His eyes flickered behind his glasses. "It's all right, Virginia. We all have our moments."

She smiled. I said, "Thanks for coming up for the game, Mom. Uh, if you don't mind, let's skip lunch." The smile turned into a frown. Wow. I didn't want to hurt her feelings. "Mom, there's something I have to do. You made me realize what."

"I did?"

"She did?" Daddy asked.

"Yes." They both stared at me expectantly. "I don't know how anything's going to turn out. I don't want to talk about it. But thanks, Mom." And I gave her a kiss.

Mom left while I washed up. Daddy was sitting in the kitchen when I came out. He sipped a glass of iced tea and looked thoughtful. "We're all making progress of a sort, aren't we?" he said.

"Yes." I didn't know what he meant about all of us,

actually, but I knew about me. I told him I was going down to the basement.

"Isn't Mrs. Heffernan there?"

"Daddy, she doesn't boil kids alive."

He laughed. She also wasn't alone. Once inside the elevator, I wondered if my plan had *any* chance of succeeding. If I understood people, *kids*, as well as I hoped I did. I had to find out.

Chapter 18

Rachel and Mrs. Heffernan were playing gin rummy. I don't know how to play. Mrs. Heffernan glanced up at me. Rachel focused on her cards.

"Am I interrupting?" I asked brilliantly. Not exactly the way I wanted to start this important conversation but all I could come up with.

"Nah, Vellars has me down two games to zip. I think she's got a system. Should take her to Atlantic City with me and let her loose at the blackjack table."

"You can't do that. She's underage."

Mrs. Heffernan rolled her eyes. Rachel snorted. The woman said, "Sit down, Matthewson. You can have the next game."

"No," Rachel and I said in unison. Redness crept into my face. Rachel continued to study the cards. "Um, I came down to see Rachel. About the kite contest."

She finally looked up but not directly at me. Sort of over my shoulder. "What about it?" she demanded.

"I promised to enter with you. I keep my promises."

"Good!" Mrs. Heffernan said. "You two can lug that junk out of my storage area. The couple in 3C is getting rid of their crib and playpen and they want it stored down here. I have to make room."

"*I'll* take the stuff up to *my* apartment after this game."

"Your stepmother's having a tea party, remember? She won't appreciate you—or Matthewson—barging in there with all that gear. Especially the paste and saw."

"And you wouldn't *dare* annoy The Fourth Mrs. Vellars, would you, Rachel?" I asked innocently.

Five minutes later, without a word spoken between us, we were in Rachel's apartment. The "poodies" yipped, her stepmother moaned, and Rachel swiped half a dozen cucumber sandwiches from the silver tray. The guests, about five women, stared popeyed at Rachel.

"Hey!" she called to her stepmother. "I didn't know you went in for playing statues."

"Oh, Rachel! I'm sorry, girls. She's just—"

But the words of The Fourth Mrs. Vellars were lost to us. We were already up the stairs and in Rachel's room.

I collapsed on a new beanbag and laughed. "That one woman had purple hair."

"Last week it was blue!" Rachel roared. Then she remembered she wasn't really friends with me and her face tightened. "Look, we finish this kite together and that's it, kiddo."

"That's it." I was hoping for more but I had to accept whatever Rachel offered. For now.

Rachel tried to stay quiet, but for her not talking is like Garfield not craving lasagna. She chattered away about the kite, giving me orders as she went along. I finished the drawings. My Leo the Lion sign ended up looking exactly like Oatmeal.

"The contest is Monday at 10:00 A.M.," she said. "You'll be there?"

"Sure, I'm the one with the good balance, remember?"

"Just checking. We'll have a dry run tomorrow."

Oh, boy. "I can't, Rachel."

"Don't tell me—you're going to the Lowerys open house."

"How'd you know? Are you bugging phones now?"

She hooted. "I'm right then. And no about the phones. Though it's an interesting idea." I looked horrified (I'm sure) and she hooted again. "Kiddo, the Lowerys give those open houses every three-day weekend. My father and his wife are always invited. They never go," she added sadly. "And I'm not about to show up alone."

"Daddy and I are going. You wouldn't be alone."

For a second, I thought she'd say yes, but she shook her head. "I got other plans." Another card game with Mrs. Heffernan?

"It's ready," she said after awhile. She was standing, tugging at the line, and feeling the wooden sticks. "She's a beaut, huh, kiddo?"

It was super looking. Rachel had been so careful making it, even if the area around us looked like a garbage dump. The kite was neat and sturdy. Totally unlike her projects for art. She had every reason to be proud. "A beaut," I said.

"You be in the park Monday before ten," she said as I got ready to leave.

"I promise."

"And you always keep your promises," she said with more than a hint of sarcasm.

I wasn't sure if Rachel was beginning to like me again or just wanted to win the contest. I wondered about winning. What would it be like? Again, I thought about the nutty contestants on *The Price Is Right* and those other game shows. They went loony when they won a piano that they probably couldn't play or didn't have room for in their homes. I wouldn't act that way. What would our prize be, anyhow? Funny. I never even asked Rachel that. She didn't seem concerned about what we won. Just that we did. Probably a cup or a ribbon. Nothing to go bananas over.

The next day, Daddy and I went to the Lowerys' open house. Beth's voice was a little croaky, but she could see people. Amanda, Frannie, and I went to her room immediately. While they talked, I played with Sleeky.

"Anything wrong, Cory?" Beth asked when Amanda and Frannie left the room for more food.

"No." Then I blurted out, "Well, you see I'm entered in tomorrow's kite flying contest—"

"That's super! We'll all come down to cheer you—"

"—with Rachel. It was her idea. She's a kite freak. But I'm having fun with it. I like being in the contest." In a whisper, I added, "And I like Rachel."

"I guess someone has to. I don't mind, you know."

"You don't?" I asked, tugging at my wispy hair. Sleeky was asleep in my lap.

"Of course not."

"But you called her gruesome. So did Amanda and Frannie."

"Cory, I don't like Maria, either, but that never

stopped me from being friends with Amanda. Amanda's terrific. She can't help it if she likes Maria." Beth wrinkled her small nose. "She says she sees something in her that I don't."

"She does? What?"

"She says Maria gets scared sometimes because her parents are real, real pushy. Maria has to get the best grades, the best clothes, the best everything—like when her aunt designed that kite for her last year. Her parents wanted her to win that contest. I don't think Maria cared one way or another." Beth pursed her lips. "I think that's dumb. Doing something you don't really want to do. I'm glad my parents aren't like that."

"Mmmmm," I murmured. Another side of Maria. Didn't I see another side of Rachel? The funny side. And how lonely she was.

"That's what Amanda tells me about Maria. I still think Maria is stuck-up and silly, but if Amanda insists she's not all bad, I believe it. I trust Amanda. And I trust you, too, Cory. If you say Rachel's not all bad, okay. But I still don't want to hang out with her," she added firmly.

"I was afraid you'd say that."

"She doesn't want to be around us, either. Doesn't she call us snobbie-creepos?" I blushed. "I rest my case."

"Maybe the next time we play fantasy-reality, you'll act out a lawyer?"

She giggled. "That's a good idea!" We heard Frannie and Amanda scampering down the hall. Beth said, "Good luck tomorrow, Cory."

I smiled. Beth was still my friend. So were the other two. I just had one other to worry about.

I was outside the Claredon at nine-thirty. I'd taken a chance and called for Rachel. Gwendolyn answered the door. "She's out. I don't know where," the housekeeper said nervously. "She took this big thing with her. I hope it's not valuable art. It looked junky enough to be that. Do you think she'll hock it?"

Gwendolyn is unreal. I told her it was a kite and she muttered, "What next?" I wondered that, too.

Some people were already in the park. I knew the contest would be held on the perimeter, away from the trees and near enough to the Hudson to catch the river breeze. Rachel was there. She was checking the line again.

"It won't fall apart. I might, but it won't."

She turned around. "Nervous, kiddo?"

"My stomach feels like your beanbag got loose in it."

I think she wanted to laugh but she held it in. She again instructed me on how to hold the reel. We went through the paces of flying the kite. It wasn't hard once I was convinced the enormous box wouldn't crash land on my small body.

After a while, I said, "I know what you mean about feeling free."

I looked at her. A man's voice suddenly boomed out, "It's now time for our annual Memorial Day kite flying contest. Will the entrants please come over to the podium?"

The podium was a makeshift stand. The kite looked sturdier than it did. A good-sized crowd had gathered. More than good-sized. Most of the people from the Claredon and Kingsley were present. My stomach galloped some more. I clutched it and moaned.

"Don't barf on me, kiddo," Rachel said sternly. But her eyes danced. She was just as excited as I was.

We were in the eight-to-thirteen group. There were only five entrants. One kite tore as soon as it went up, another wouldn't get off the ground. Jenny Chee had a beautifully painted kite, but she had a terrible time holding onto it. Finally, her father had to race after it and catch it before it blew into the river. The fourth kite was handsome, and the boy flew it well.

"Don't get bent out of shape, kiddo. Ours has more style."

"Style? With my Sagittarius looking like Cupid and the lion the spitting image of Oatmeal?"

She didn't answer. The man in charge announced us. Daddy yelled, "Way to go, Cory!" Then he added, "Rachel, too."

"C'mon," I urged when she wouldn't budge. "Don't tell me you have stage fright?"

"Nah, it was just hearing your old man. My old man and The Fourth Mrs. Vellars went to the Hamptons."

"My mom went away, too," I said quickly. "C'mon, Rachel. We have to fly the kite."

"Right. We're going to win." She turned to the crowd. "Listen up, folks. This is a box kite and those gorgeous designs are signs of the zodiac. I did all the heavy work. Cory was the artist. She's also going to fly it since she's Little Miss Twinkletoes and never trips over her teeny footsies. Go ahead, folks. Give my— uh, Cory, a big hand."

They did, but I was more concerned with what Rachel hadn't said. I'm positive she was about to say, "my friend." There was a chance! I needed her friendship.

But I couldn't think about that now. It was kite flying time. And after Rachel's crazy introduction, I made sure I didn't trip. The kite soared aloft. It was a breathtaking sight. I kept it up for three minutes then reeled it in with Rachel's help.

Then there was silence. Rachel kept hopping from one foot to the other. "We've got it made, kiddo."

I didn't say anything. My mouth was all dry. Second prize was a bright, satin ribbon. First prize was a big cup. The man in charge said the winners' names would be engraved at a later date.

Second prize went to the boy with the gorgeous kite. I knew we had to win.

"And first prize goes to the wonderful box kite made by Rachel Vellars and Cory Matthewson."

I don't know what happened to me then. Just like the contestants on *The Price Is Right*, I began bouncing around. I looked at Rachel. She was absolutely still. How could that be?

From the corner of my eye, I spotted Daddy coming through the crowd. "We did it!" I hollered at the top of my lungs. I hadn't yelled that way since I fell off a swing in Manhattan and cut both knees and bruised my forehead.

"Rachel, you said we'd win and we did. We did it!" I pranced around, just the way Rachel always did. Except that Rachel was standing perfectly still, holding the cup the man had presented her.

"Daddy! We won! My best friend and I won it

together!" Daddy grinned. I looked at Rachel again. She was gawking at me. I suddenly threw my arms around her, hugged her, got slightly stabbed by the cup's handle, but didn't care, and hugged her again.

When I finally let go, her eyes were watery. She shook her head, smiled, and in a quivery voice said, "Cory Matthewson, how could you?"

After graduating from business school, Lois I. Fisher worked in many fields, including fashion, magazine publishing, and construction. Her favorite was working on the construction site of a Manhattan skyscraper.

Her hobbies include watching sports, doing difficult crossword puzzles, and collecting rock records from the 1960s.

Stories by Lois Fisher have appeared in dozens of juvenile and young adult publications. She is the author of several novels, including *Wretched Robert* and *Puffy P. Pushycat, Problem Solver*. She lives in The Bronx, New York.